Rachel Renée Russell

DORK diaries

Frenemies Forever

with Nikki Russell and Erin Russell

SIMON & SCHUSTER

This paperback edition published 2017
First published in Great Britain in 2016 by Simon and Schuster UK Ltd
A CBS COMPANY

First published in the USA in 2016 as Dork Diaries 11: Tales from a
Not-So-Friendly Frenemy by Aladdin, an imprint of Simon & Schuster Children's Publishing Division.

Copyright © 2016 Rachel Renée Russell
Series design by Lisa Vega
The text of this book was set in Skippy Sharp and Beautiful Every Time

1 3 5 7 9 10 8 6 4 2

Simon & Schuster UK Ltd
1st Floor, 222 Gray's Inn Road
London WC1X 8HB

Simon & Schuster Australia, Sydney
Simon & Schuster India, New Delhi

www.simonandschuster.co.uk
www.simonandschuster.com.au
www.simonandschuster.co.in

www.dorkdiaries.co.uk

A CIP catalogue record for this book
is available from the British Library.

PB ISBN: 978-1-4711-5804-9
eBook ISBN: 978-1-4711-5802-5

Printed and bound by CPI Group (UK) Ltd, Croydon, CR0 4YY

MIX
Paper from
responsible sources
FSC® C020471

Simon & Schuster UK Ltd are committed to sourcing paper
that is made from wood grown in sustainable forests and support the Forest
Stewardship Council, the leading international forest certification organisation.
Our books displaying the FSC logo are printed on FSC certified paper.

To Camryn Chase

You're a star! Keep dancing!

NOOOOOO ☹!!

I CAN'T believe this is actually happening to me!!

I just found out yesterday that I'm going to be attending North Hampton Hills International Academy for one week as part of a student exchange program!

Yes, I know. It's a VERY prestigious school, known for its outstanding students, rigorous academics, chic uniforms, and beautiful campus that's a twist between Hogwarts and a five-star luxury hotel!

Most students would give up their CELL PHONES for a chance to attend there.

So WHY am I totally FREAKING OUT?!!

Because it's ALSO the school that a certain DRAMA QUEEN just transferred to ☹!

Yes, it's true! Unfortunately . . .

MACKENZIE HOLLISTER ATTENDS
NORTH HAMPTON HILLS!

Calling her a mean girl is an understatement. She's a RATTLESNAKE in lip gloss and hoop earrings and blond hair extensions. . . .

I have no idea why she HATES my GUTS!

But you'll NEVER believe THIS!

According to the latest gossip (from her little sister, Amanda, to my little sister, Brianna), a few of the North Hampton Hills girls have actually been HATING on MacKenzie! . . .

THEY MADE FUN OF MACKENZIE
BECAUSE OF THAT VIDEO
WITH THE BUG IN HER HAIR!

AND WENT OUT OF THEIR WAY
TO MAKE HER LIFE MISERABLE!

But all of this gets even STRANGER!

I saw MacKenzie a few days ago at the CupCakery,
and she was hanging out with some of her new
friends. PRETENDING to be . . . ME!

It was so BIZARRE, I almost flipped out! I wanted to rush down to the local POLICE STATION and scream . . .

HELP ME, PLEASE! IT'S AN EMERGENCY! MY IDENTITY HAS BEEN STOLEN!!

We hope you enjoy this book.
Please return or renew it by the due date.
You can renew it at **www.norfolk.gov.uk/libraries**
or by using our free library app. Otherwise you can
phone **0344 800 8020** - please have your library
card and pin ready.
You can sign up for email reminders too.

2nd March

16. AUG 21.

08. AUG 22

10. DEC 18

18 04 19

ALSO BY
Rachel Renée Russell

DORK DIARIES

THE MISADVENTURES OF MAX CRUMBLY

Thanks to MacKenzie, my life is a never-ending

DRAMAFEST!!

In just the past month or so, she has:

1. slammed me in the face with a dodgeball

2. stolen my diary

3. hacked into my newspaper advice column

4. accused me of cyberbullying her

AND

5. pretended to be ME.

Like, WHO does that?!!

Only a complete and utter . . .

SICKO!

After MacKenzie transferred, I was hoping I'd NEVER have to see her face again.

But NOOOO!!!

Next week I'll be stuck attending North Hampton Hills with a spiteful, lip-gloss-addicted IDENTITY THIEF ☹!

PLEASE, PLEASE, PLEASE let my BFFs, Chloe and Zoey, get assigned to that school too.

With them by my side, I can get through just about ANYTHING!

Including a PAINFULLY long, MISERABLE week with my WORST enemy!

☹!

I just got to school a few minutes ago, and the eighth-grade students are already buzzing about Student Exchange Week.

I'm dying to talk to Chloe and Zoey about it.

But right now I'm so SLEEPY I can barely keep my eyes open.

Yesterday my parents surprised me with a . . .

NEW PUPPY!

Yes, it's true! The Maxwell family has a dog!

Her name is Daisy, and she's a golden retriever.

She's a sweet, happy, wiggly bundle of energy.

I LOVE her SO much that I'm thinking about making a new designer fragrance for teens called . . .

9

PUPPY BREATH!!

Daisy is absolutely PERFECT ☺!! She's SUPERplayful and so silly that she makes me laugh.

Anyway, I was so stressed out about having to attend North Hampton Hills that I barely got any sleep last night.

Although Daisy didn't help matters. As much as I adore her, I'm starting to wish she had an ON/OFF switch, because . . .

THAT DOG NEVER SLEEPS!

And every time I drifted off to sleep, she'd get bored and lonely and want to PLAY. . . .

DAISY DECIDES TO WAKE ME UP!

By SCARING the SNOT out of me!

ME, BEING ATTACKED BY A FEROCIOUS
FURBALL IN THE MIDDLE OF THE NIGHT!

She was so cute that I couldn't stay mad. . . .

ME, SNUGGLING WITH DAISY
(AND TRYING TO GET HER TO SLEEP!)

OMG! I probably got LESS than seventeen minutes of sleep the ENTIRE night!

It's Daisy's fault that I'm tired and grumpy and will be SLEEPWALKING from class to class.

I'm almost too exhausted to even WORRY about Student Exchange Week.

I wish it were a REAL foreign exchange student program for some faraway, exotic place, like maybe . . . Paris, France!

I'd **LOVE, LOVE, LOVE** to spend a week in PARIS ☺! It's SUCH a romantic city!

I just turned in a project for French class about the Louvre art museum, which contains some of the world's most famous masterpieces.

I hope I get a decent grade on it since my report and hand-drawn illustrations took me FOREVER to complete!

Anyway, I just had the most brilliant idea!

Since I'm a library shelving assistant, I can use that as an EXCUSE to get out of the program.

I'll simply ~~ask~~ BEG our librarian, Mrs. Peach, to let me ~~hang out~~ HELP OUT in the library during Student Exchange Week.

School will be out for the summer soon, and there's a ton of work that needs to be done to get the library ready for next year.

So I am pretty sure she'll say yes.

PROBLEM SOLVED! RIGHT ☺?!

WRONG ☹!!

That's when Principal Winston made an announcement over the PA system about Student Exchange Week. He explained that the final week of the program would start on Monday, May 12, and those of us eighth-graders who hadn't already participated in a previous week would be receiving a letter with details about our host school assignment later today.

He reminded us that instead of being graded on class assignments, students will receive one credit for successfully completing the program. Any student failing to do so will end up one credit short for completing eighth grade and _NOT_ be promoted to ninth grade!

As if all of that news wasn't **BAD** enough, he said the credit would have to be made up by attending SUMMER SCHOOL!

SORRY!! But as much as I HATE the thought of spending a week with MacKenzie, I HATE the thought of spending the ENTIRE summer in school EVEN MORE ☹!

This student exchange program was quickly turning into a MASSIVE HEADACHE!

Even though I felt overwhelmed, I decided to handle my problem in a very calm and mature manner.

17

So I went straight to the girls' bathroom. . . .

And had a COMPLETE MELTDOWN!!

☹!!

We just received our letters. . . .

FROM THE OFFICE OF
PRINCIPAL WINSTON

TO: Nikki Maxwell

FROM: Principal Winston

RE: EIGHTH-GRADE STUDENT EXCHANGE WEEK

Dear Nikki,

Each year, all eighth-grade students at Westchester Country Day Middle School participate in Student Exchange Week with local schools. We feel this helps to foster community and good citizenship between students and faculty at the host schools. Participation is mandatory for YOU to meet your eighth-grade requirements.

Next week you will be attending NORTH HAMPTON HILLS INTERNATIONAL ACADEMY (NHH). You are expected to be on your best behavior and follow the NHH handbook. Photos for student IDs will be taken on Friday, May 9.

If you have any questions or concerns, please feel free to contact me.

Sincerely,

PRINCIPAL WINSTON

19

Everyone was excitedly reading their letters and discussing their school assignments.

Principal Winston had also placed the master list right outside the office door.

I was at my locker writing in my diary when Chloe and Zoey rushed up to me, happily waving their letters in the air.

"OMG, Nikki! Guess what?! WE have the SAME school!" Chloe shrieked hysterically.

"WHAT?! NO WAY!" I blinked in surprise. "WE DO?! Are you sure?!"

I assumed that Chloe and Zoey had already checked the office list for my assignment.

"Chloe's right!" Zoey smiled. "WE'RE assigned to the same school! Can you believe it?!"

That news was almost too good to be true. I smiled and breathed a sigh of relief.

I had wasted all that energy worrying for no reason.

I was FINALLY starting to feel excited about the exchange program. It might actually be FUN!

"We're going to have a BLAST!" Chloe squealed. "Group hug, everyone!"

We were doing a group hug when Brandon walked up.

"Let me guess. The three of you have been assigned to the same school! Right?!" He smiled.

"YEP! So, what school did YOU get?" Zoey asked.

When Brandon held up his letter, Chloe and Zoey both screeched, "OMG!! BRANDON HAS THE SAME SCHOOL AS US!"

"This is KA-RAY-ZEE!" I giggled happily. "It seems almost UNBELIEVABLE that the FOUR of us have been assigned to—"

ME, FEELING TOTALLY CONFUSED!

"WHAT?!" I gasped in shock. "Wait a minute, guys! Are you sure?!"

But Chloe, Zoey, and Brandon didn't seem to hear me. The three of them were laughing and talking about how GREAT it was going to be to hang out with Brandon's best friend, Max Crumbly, at South Ridge Middle School.

Suddenly my stomach started to churn and I could taste the breakfast burrito I had eaten this morning. I bit my lip and tried to swallow the lump in my throat.

No one seemed to notice that I was upset. It was like I was invisible or something. And these people were SUPPOSED to be my FRIENDS?!

I didn't have any choice but to ask myself a very difficult question. . . .

WHY DID I FEEL LIKE A . . . GIANT BUCKET OF . . .

PUKE?!!! . . .

Suddenly everyone stopped talking and stared at me.
"Nikki, are you okay?!"

That's when I closed my eyes and wailed. . . .

"MACKENZIE'S SCHOOL?!" they gasped.

I totally lost it right there in front of my locker as my three friends watched helplessly.

"That's TERRIBLE!" Chloe groaned.

"You POOR thing!" Zoey moaned.

"What CRUDDY luck!" Brandon muttered.

OMG!

I was so frustrated and angry, I wanted to . . .

SCREAM!!

There's just NO WAY I'm attending school with MacKenzie only to be publicly humiliated by her.

AGAIN!!

I guess this means I'll be signing up for summer school.

Sorry, Principal Winston!

But now that I know none of my friends will be at NHH with me, I'd rather poke my eye out with a dirty stick than be in your STUPID program!

☹!!

MONDAY—1:45 P.M.
IN BIOLOGY CLASS

Brandon and I are lab partners in bio and sit next to each other. I guess he must be worried about me or something, because he's been texting me nonstop. . . .

BRANDON: R U OK?

NIKKI: I'm fine. Just a little bummed out about the NHH fiasco.

BRANDON: How about I talk 2 Principal Winston about us switching schools?

NIKKI: ???

BRANDON: U go to South Ridge with BFFs. I go 2 Hogwarts. Then will U smile again?

NIKKI: R U kidding me? U would do that?!

BRANDON: Sure! 4 a friend.

NIKKI: Thanx! But I'm OK now. 4 real!

We stared at our text messages and blushed. Then we stared at each other and blushed. All of this staring and blushing went on, like, FOREVER! . . .

BRANDON AND ME, TEXTING IN BIO

BRANDON: This class is so boring.

NIKKI: Totally agree. I'm trying to stay awake.

BRANDON: If I doze off, please SLAP me.

NIKKI: OK. LOL! Stop making me laugh or we'll both get detentions for texting in class.

BRANDON: Hey, at least U R smiling again!

By the time bio was over, Brandon had cheered me up. I was starting to feel like maybe it WASN'T the end of the world after all.

It was really sweet of him to offer to trade places with me and attend NHH. But MacKenzie has an even bigger CRUSH on Brandon than I do! She would happily give up lip gloss for the rest of her life to spend an entire week hanging out with him at NHH.

Sorry, girlfriend! But that is so NOT happening!

☺!!

MONDAY—7:00 P.M.
AT HOME

I was SO relieved when the school day was finally
OVER!

It seemed to drag on FOREVER!

I really can't blame Chloe, Zoey, and Brandon for
being excited about the student exchange program.

Hey, I'd be excited about it too if I were attending
South Ridge Middle School.

The last thing I want is for my friends to ~~know~~
think I'm having a huge PITY PARTY just because
I'm stuck attending North Hampton Hills with
MacKenzie.

Anyway, when I finally got home from school, my
bratty little sister, Brianna, was in the kitchen
working on a Scouting project.

It seems like she's been trying to earn a cooking

badge, like, FOREVER. But, unfortunately,
everything she makes turns out just AWFUL! . . .

BRIANNA, COOKING UP A REALLY HUGE MESS!

My curiosity finally got the best of me.

"Hi, Brianna! So, what are you making this time?" I asked.

"I've FINALLY perfected my chocolate pudding recipe!" Brianna exclaimed happily. "Now I just need to bake it for one hour."

"Actually, I don't think it's necessary to BAKE chocolate pudding. You should put it in the FRIDGE for one hour," I suggested.

"I'M the chef, and it's MY recipe! I say it goes in the OVEN for one hour! So THERE!" she said, and stuck her tongue out at me.

I just rolled my eyes at that girl.

But what did I expect from a spoiled wannabe chef who secretly uses boogers when she runs out of cupcake sprinkles?

Anyway, about forty minutes later I noticed a really foul odor. It kind of smelled like a garbage dump. On fire!

I rushed into the kitchen to check on Brianna.

"Nikki, take a look at my masterpiece!" She grinned as she held it out for me to see. . . .

"Doesn't this look DELISH?!!"

Brianna's "masterpiece" looked like a puddle of black tar with macaroni and several eyeballs stuck in it!

I actually threw up in my mouth! EWWW ☹!!

"I made this snack especially for my Scout meeting today. And if the girls like it, I'll finally earn my cooking badge!" she explained.

"Well, everyone loves, um . . . BURNT chocolate pudding, right?! YUM YUM!!" I stammered. "And it smells. Really strong. So, good luck with your badge."

"Thanks! I also added eggs for a crunchy texture," she said. "I learned that from the Chef's Choice TV show."

"You were supposed to CRACK the eggs first, NOT toss them in whole," I said.

"But the eggshells are the yummy crunchy part! Would you like to try some of my pudding? You're gonna LOVE it!" . . .

BRIANNA, TRYING TO SHOVE HER PUDDING
DOWN MY THROAT!

OMG! That's when I threw up inside my mouth
again ☹!!

Unless Brianna's cooking skills drastically improved, I FEARED for the nutritional health of her future husband and children. . . .

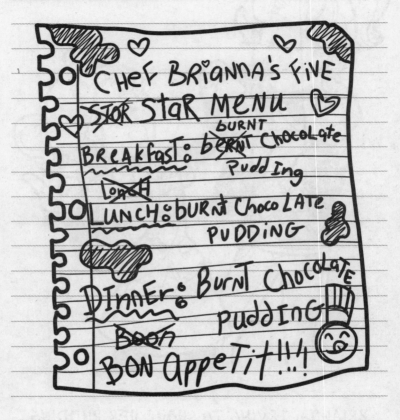

BRIANNA'S MENU FOR HER FAMILY

OMG! HOW were they going to SURVIVE on a diet of BURNT chocolate pudding?!!

But I felt even SORRIER for those poor little girls who would be eating Brianna's pudding as a snack later.

Their frantic parents would be rushing them straight to the emergency room as soon as the Scout meeting was over.

WHY?

Because the entire troop would need to get their STOMACHS PUMPED due to Brianna's NASTY chocolate pudding.

The good news was that maybe she could have earned a stomach pump badge.

Anyway, when Brianna arrived back home from her Scout meeting, she was visibly upset.

"How did things go?" I asked.

"TERRIBLE! Everyone HATED my chocolate pudding!" she grumbled.

"Well, your pudding dish is empty. So even if the girls complained a little, they liked it enough to have eaten ALL of it!"

"No, they DIDN'T! After our troop leader contacted Poison Control, we were advised to dig a deep hole in the woods and bury the leftovers," Brianna ranted.

"Bury it in the woods?! But why?!" I asked.

"So no human or animal would accidentally EAT it. By the end of the meeting, we'd all earned our safety with toxic substances badge."

"Well, at least you and your troop earned a new badge. That's a GOOD thing, right?"

"WRONG! I was completely HUMILIATED!" Brianna sulked.

I didn't want to hurt Brianna's feelings, but it was true. Her pudding was better suited for filling potholes in the street than for human consumption.

"I'll NEVER earn a cooking badge!" Brianna sighed. "I'm the WORST cook EVER!!"

Brianna WAS the worst cook ever!

But she was also my little sister, and I didn't want to see her dream of earning a cooking badge destroyed.

I felt really bad for Brianna.

It seemed like only yesterday that I was six years old and totally obsessed with baking tiny burnt cupcakes in my very own Easy-Bake Oven.

I decided to talk to my parents about all of this.

But first I gave Brianna a big HUG!

Then I made her a huge bowl of her fave dessert— ice cream, ketchup, and raisins—to cheer her up.

BRIANNA EATS HER FAVE DESSERT
OF ICE CREAM, KETCHUP, AND RAISINS

It TOTALLY worked ☺!!

Within minutes she was smiling from ear to ear ☺!

But watching her actually EAT that stuff was
DISGUSTING! I just threw up in my mouth for the
THIRD time this evening.

EWWW!! ☹!!

TUESDAY, MAY 6—NOON
IN THE LIBRARY

I'm STILL totally stressed out about Student Exchange Week.

I dreaded attending North Hampton Hills because it meant dealing with MacKenzie and her crazy, mean-girl drama.

But if I DIDN'T participate, I'd be forced to make up the lost credit by attending summer school.

My situation was HOPELESS ☹!

Thank goodness Chloe, Zoey, and I had PE together during fourth period. I finally decided to talk to them about my problem.

Since the weather was nice, our class went outside on the soccer field to work on drills. The three of us took turns dribbling our balls around a set of plastic cones while discussing my latest life crisis. . . .

41

ME AND MY BFFS, DOING SOCCER DRILLS
AND DISCUSSING MY LATEST LIFE CRISIS

"Listen, Nikki, if you don't want to attend MacKenzie's school, maybe you should just explain your reason to Principal Winston," Zoey suggested. "I'm sure he'd understand."

"I totally agree," Chloe added. "If people knew even half of the AWFUL things that girl has done, no school would accept her as a student. Heck, her OWN parents would even REFUSE to HOMESCHOOL her!"

"I don't know, guys," I sighed. "MacKenzie stole my diary and kept it for twelve days! Remember? There was a lot of SUPERpersonal stuff in there that I wouldn't want ANYONE to know, especially Principal Winston."

"I think it's about time you stood up for yourself, Nikki!" Chloe argued. "You can't let MacKenzie continue to get away with the things she has been doing!"

After agonizing over my situation for what seemed like forever, I finally made up my mind. I knew exactly what I needed to do. . . .

43

44

"Thanks, guys! You're the best friends EVER! I know I need to do this. But just the thought of dealing with MacKenzie and her drama makes me SICK to my stomach!" I grumbled.

"Even if MacKenzie gets mad at you, what can she do?! TATTLE about some of the trivial stuff she read in your diary? Big fat hairy deal! At worst, you might get a few days of after-school detention," Chloe fumed.

Wait a minute!! A few days of DETENTION?!

"Yeah, it won't be the end of the world," Zoey agreed. "You'll get over it!"

Sorry, but it WILL be the end of MY world!! When my parents KILL ME ☹!

I could NOT believe my BFFs could be so insensitive.

"So . . . you both realize I didn't just write about the CRAZY stuff I did. I ALSO wrote about the CRAZY stuff WE did." I reminded them about . . .

Joyriding in the library . . .

Making prank calls on the school phone . . .

Sneaking into the boys' locker room . . .

Pretending to be on the football team . . .

Wandering the halls with a garbage can instead of a hall pass . . .

SQUEAK!!
SQUEAK!!

Smuggling eight dogs into the school . . .

← DOGS

BOOKS
FOR
LIBRARY

AND the fact that we've been SECRETLY
hanging out in the JANITOR'S CLOSET, like,
FOREVER. . . .

"That's not even everything we've done," I ranted. "Forget detention. WE'LL probably get a one-week SUSPENSION!"

Suddenly Chloe and Zoey got really quiet.

They both stared at me in total disbelief.

"Did you j—just say 'WE'?!" Zoey finally sputtered.

"Um, on second thought, reporting MacKenzie might NOT be the best way to handle things," Chloe muttered. "Did I mention that I'm ALLERGIC to suspensions?"

Okay, now I was starting to get a little ticked off.

I know Chloe and Zoey are supposed to be my BFFs. But it seemed like they thought ratting on MacKenzie was a really good idea until they realized that they might end up getting in TROUBLE along with me.

"So NOW you both think talking to Principal Winston might NOT be such a good idea after all? Then what am I supposed to do about Student Exchange Week?"

"Well, Nikki, you can always try to look on the bright side," Zoey offered.

"There ISN'T a bright side!" I grumped.

"Sure there is!" Zoey grinned. "You'll finally know what it's like to attend Hogwarts, but without the MAGIC classes!"

"Yeah, and their school uniforms are classy, chic, and SUPERcute!!" Chloe giggled.

I just rolled my eyes. Chloe and Zoey were no help WHATSOEVER!!

If I'm really lucky, maybe I'll find some NEW BFFs at North Hampton Hills!

☹!!

OMG! OMG! OMG!

I CANNOT believe what just happened to me in French class today (which, BTW, I had during seventh period due to standardized testing)!!

I'm so FREAKED OUT right now I can barely write this!

My heart is POUNDING, and it feels like my head is about to EXPLODE!

MUST. CALM. DOWN!!

It all started when my French teacher, Monsieur Dupont, returned my report about the Louvre, the world-famous art museum located in Paris.

It was seven typed pages and included several detailed illustrations that I'd personally drawn. I almost FAINTED when I saw my grade. . . .

ME, SHOCKED AND SURPRISED THAT
I GOT AN A+ ON MY REPORT!

I know, right?

But when my teacher asked me to stay after class because he wanted to talk to me about my report, I started to panic.

What if he thought I had cheated on it by plagiarizing or something ☹?!

I could understand why he might have been a little suspicious.

I'm definitely NOT the best student in his class, and I have to work really hard just to get a B.

But I actually ENJOYED writing my report!

I was SUPERinspired and motivated because the topic was art, and I really LOVE art!

Anyway, after class I went up to talk to my teacher.

I was really nervous and my stomach felt queasy.

But mostly I was praying I wouldn't THROW UP all over his desk! . . .

ME, TALKING TO MY TEACHER
ABOUT MY REPORT?!

Thank goodness THAT didn't happen!

Instead, I stood there clutching my report while my teacher raved about how impressed he was with my work. Then things got a little strange.

"Nikki, I think you'd be PERFECT for an honors French program this summer. You're such a talented artist, and the program's focus is art history and French culture. Would you be interested in participating?"

"Well, is it the ENTIRE summer?" I asked hesitantly. I did NOT want to attend summer school.

"I think it's about ten days in August. A group of students from area schools will be traveling to Paris to visit the Louvre and other historical landmarks!"

That's when I almost fainted.

AGAIN!!

"OMG! Did you just say a TRIP TO PARIS TO VISIT THE LOUVRE?!" I screeched excitedly. "YES! I'D LOVE TO GO TO PARIS!!"

"Great! The only slight complication is that the all-expenses-paid trip is being sponsored by the foreign languages department at North Hampton Hills International Academy. So I need to contact them to get all the details. But I'd be happy to recommend you for the program."

Guess what?! I almost fainted a THIRD time when he mentioned North Hampton Hills!

"Actually, Monsieur Dupont, I'm supposed to be attending North Hampton Hills next week as part of our Student Exchange Week!"

"PERFECT! Then I'll contact their foreign languages department and arrange for you to follow up with them while you're there visiting. I'll also forward a copy of your report and artwork. I'm sure they will be as impressed as I am."

"Thank you SO much for considering me!" I gushed.
"It's such a wonderful opportunity!"

Then I calmly walked out of the classroom and
gleefully did my Snoopy "happy dance" all the way
back to my locker. . . .

ME, DOING MY SNOOPY "HAPPY DANCE"

SQUEEEEEEEE ☺!!

I can't believe I might actually be going to

PARIS, FRANCE!! . . .

... AS AN INTERNATIONAL EXCHANGE
STUDENT!

So now I need to really impress the North Hampton
Hills foreign languages department. They need to
know that I'm smart, disciplined, dedicated, and an
outstanding student.

Well, okay. Maybe I'm NOT all of those things!

But I AM interested in learning more about art history and French culture. And I'm nice, I'm friendly, and EVERYONE likes me.

Well, okay. Maybe not EVERYONE. And by "not everyone," I mean people like . . .

MACKENZIE HOLLISTER ☹!!

Anyway, I can't wait to tell Chloe and Zoey the wonderful news! They're going to FREAK!!

I thought my week at North Hampton Hills was going to be DOOM, GLOOM, and DREAD! But I was SO wrong!

It's going to be FANTASTIC!

WEDNESDAY, MAY 7—5:30 P.M.
AT HOME

Chloe and Zoey were SUPERhappy for me when
I told them the unbelievable news about Monsieur
Dupont and the possible trip to Paris. Yesterday
we talked on the phone and then texted each
other until almost midnight.

And today I received even MORE exciting news
during lunch!

It was a delivery confirmation e-mail that my
North Hampton Hills SCHOOL UNIFORM had just
been delivered to my house.

SQUEEEEE ☺!!

I'll just be borrowing the uniform for one week and
then returning it to the school. But STILL ☺!
Chloe, Zoey, and I were so excited.

"I'll text you photos as soon as I try it on!" I told
them as we ate lunch.

But they insisted on coming over to my house after school to hang out, and I agreed.

As soon as Chloe and Zoey saw the box, they immediately started SPAZZING OUT. . . .

They were acting like I was opening a birthday present or something.

"Come on, guys!" I giggled. "CHILLAX! It's just a uniform."

But OMG! My new uniform was . . .

AWESOME!

I have to admit, when I first saw MacKenzie in her uniform, I was SUPERimpressed.

She looked SO smart and mature.

And nothing at all like the shallow, lip-gloss-addicted DRAMA QUEEN that she really is.

MacKenzie is going to be very shocked and surprised to see ME at HER school on Monday.

But I plan to ignore her and stay focused.

My major goal is to snag that trip to Paris!

And absolutely NOTHING—not even MacKenzie Hollister—is going to stand in my way!

I put on MY uniform and stood in front of the mirror with a huge smile plastered on my face.

I thought it looked really sharp on me.

And my BFFs totally agreed! . . .

CHLOE AND ZOEY, ADMIRING
MY CLASSY NHH SCHOOL UNIFORM

Then I got an unexpected SURPRISE!

My BFFs told me how proud they were of me and gave me a pink sparkly gift bag with the Eiffel Tower on it.

Inside was a box of Godiva chocolates, an English-to-French translation book of common phrases (like "Where is the bathroom?"), and the newest issue of *That's So Hot!* magazine.

"Nikki, this mag has great tips on being an international exchange student! It'll help you prepare for your trip!" Chloe explained.

I thanked my BFFs for the gifts and for always being there for me. Then I gave them both a big hug.

I'm already starting to miss them, and I haven't even left for North Hampton Hills yet.

Chloe and Zoey are the BEST. FRIENDS. EVER!! ☺!

I DREAD taking school photos! But tomorrow is picture day for everyone participating in Student Exchange Week.

We have to report to the WCD library during first period to take photos for our student IDs, which we are required to have for the program.

In geometry class my teacher was at the board figuring out a problem using the Pythagorean theorem.

But I was at my desk trying to figure out a much more complex problem. WHAT was I going to wear in my photo?

I pulled out my new *That's So Hot!* magazine and placed it on top of my math book. I was flipping through the fashion section for ideas when I spotted an ad. . . .

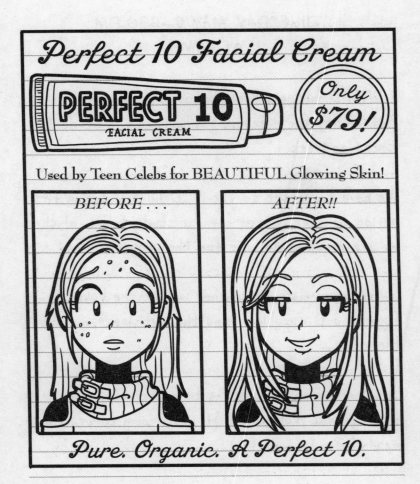

Hey, I wasn't STUPID!

Everyone knows the "before" and "after" photos in these types of ads are totally FAKE.

Which also means Perfect 10 facial cream is probably FAKE.

But the ad also said "Used by Teen Celebs for Beautiful Glowing Skin!"

And if it's good enough for THEM, then it's good enough for ME!

I was amazed to discover that not only is Perfect 10 pure and organic, but it's made from fancy ingredients like honey, plain Greek yogurt, blueberry extract, grape-seed oil, figs, seaweed, moon dust, and spring water.

OMG! I am DYING to try it!

Although I am fine with my dorky cuteness, I would much rather be mistaken for a glam teen celeb by people at North Hampton Hills ☺.

The only problem was that Perfect 10 is $79!

YIKES ☹!!

Sorry, but I was NOT about to let money stand in the way of achieving my dream!

I decided to create my very OWN Perfect 10 facial cream! But my cheap knockoff is going to be made from ingredients my mom already has in her kitchen. And instead of costing $79, it's basically FREE ☺!

Who knows, my very creative and ingenious idea might one day make me a BILLIONAIRE! . . .

THE DORKY GIRL'S HOMEMADE FACIAL CREAM FOR GORGEOUS GLOWING SKIN

WHAT YOU'RE <u>NOT</u> GOING TO NEED:

Are you basically BROKE, with a life savings of $3.58 secretly hidden in your sock drawer?

Is your mom adamantly REFUSING to give you $79 for Perfect 10 because she says she'd rather use the money to buy GROCERIES since your family can't EAT facial cream for dinner?

If you answered YES to either of these questions, then below is a list of the things you WON'T need.

I've already crossed out EVERYTHING on this list FOR you!

You're WELCOME ☺!!

~~Honey, Greek yogurt (plain), blueberry extract, grape-seed oil, figs, seaweed, moon dust, and natural spring water.~~

WHAT YOU'RE GOING TO NEED:

To keep things simple and save money, you'll be using ingredients you ALREADY have in your kitchen.

INGREDIENTS NEEDED
FOR THE DORKY GIRL'S
HOMEMADE FACIAL CREAM

Instead of honey, use pancake syrup.

Instead of plain Greek yogurt and blueberry extract, use Princess Sugar Plum Very Blueberry yogurt cups.

Instead of grape-seed oil, use grape juice.

Instead of figs, use fig snack cookie thingies.

Instead of seaweed, use canned spinach.

Instead of moon dust, use one package of Missy's hot cocoa mix.

Instead of spring water, use water from your kitchen faucet along with six ice cubes.

DORKY GIRL'S 10 STEPS TO BEAUTY

STEP 1: Sneak into the kitchen after your parents go to bed. Then they won't be all up in your business and asking you STUPID questions, like "Are you going to PAY for all the food you're wasting?"

STEP 2: Dump three blueberry yogurts into a large mixing bowl and put the empty containers back in the fridge so no one will suspect that YOU stole used them <evil grin>.

STEP 3: Stir in one cup of grape juice and a half cup of pancake syrup.

STEP 4: Eat the crust off six fig snack cookie thingies and add the fig stuffing to the mixture in the bowl.

STEP 5: Add in one teaspoon of cocoa mix and one tablespoon of canned spinach.

STEP 6: Stir the mixture for three minutes and then let it sit for ten minutes. Be aware that it may attract flies, and shoo them away.

STEP 7: Chillax and enjoy a cool, refreshing cup of ice water, because you've probably worked up a sweat and are pretty thirsty by now!

STEP 8: Smear the homemade facial cream all over

your face and let it dry. If there are any dead flies stuck to your face, remove them immediately for sanitary reasons.

STEP 9: Store leftovers in a covered container in the fridge for six additional facials. Or pour contents into a blender and blend on high for sixty seconds for a delicious Very Blueberry smoothie.

STEP 10: Go to bed and get plenty of beauty rest. When you wake up in the morning, remove your facial cream with warm water and a soft cloth.

You will be AWESTRUCK by the BEAUTIFUL, GLOWING, and RADIANT reflection in your mirror!

My miraculous homemade facial cream seems to be working, because my skin is tingling.

I ALREADY look and feel more beautiful ☺!! . . .

MY HOMEMADE FACIAL CREAM!

I can hardly wait to see the final results!

SQUEEEEEE ☺!!

Now it's time for ME to get some beauty rest.

When Brandon sees me tomorrow, he'll hopefully
be so captivated by my magical, mystical, and
miraculous BEAUTY that he'll profess his undying
LOVE for me.

Or at least notice that my zits have cleared up!
☺!!

As soon as my alarm clock went off this morning, I hopped out of bed, giddy with excitement! I couldn't wait to see my beautiful, glowing, radiant skin.

I thought for sure I'd look like I belonged on the cover of *Teen Vogue* magazine.

I rushed into my bathroom, washed my face with warm water, and glanced in the mirror.

That's when I heard a very familiar voice screaming in horror!

Unfortunately, the voice was MINE.

I was screaming because my face was . . .

NEON BLUE!!

OMG! I looked like PAPA SMURF'S long-lost, half-human, very homely DAUGHTER. . . .

ME, IN THE MIRROR SCREAMING!!

I wanted GLOWING skin!

Not GLOW-IN-THE-DARK skin!

I was in complete shock and just kept shrieking,

"OMG! OMG! OMG! I'M BLUE! I'M BLUE!"

I guessed that it was from all those artificial colors in Brianna's Very Blueberry yogurt and the grape juice.

I tried scrubbing my face with soap, but the bright blue color would NOT come off!

My first thought was to give up and stay home.

I could spend the entire day just sitting on my bed, staring at the wall and SULKING ☹!

Which, for some reason, always makes me feel better ☺!

But that was not an option. I needed to take that student ID photo or I wouldn't be allowed to attend North Hampton Hills.

My chance to go to Paris would be RUINED ☹!!

I scrounged around in the hall closet until I found my dad's weird-looking SKI MASK that he wore while snowblowing during blizzards.

I didn't have a choice but to wear it to school to hide my blue face ☹!

I quickly got dressed and snuck into the kitchen, carefully avoiding my family members, and grabbed a cereal bar.

OMG! If Brianna saw me in that ski mask, my life was going to be in immediate DANGER!

Brianna would take one look at me, scream

"BURGLAR!"

and then violently attack me with a frying pan.

And until my bruises healed, I'd be black and blue!

And, um . . . BLUE!

How bizarre would THAT be?!

Anyway, when I arrived at school, every single student in the hall just stopped and stared.

Between my chic outfit and my dad's ski mask, I looked like a wannabe burglar with a wicked sense of fashion. I finally made it past all the gawkers to the janitor's closet and texted Chloe and Zoey. . . .

NIKKI: HELP!! EMERGENCY!! I'M IN THE JANITOR'S CLOSET!

Very soon Chloe and Zoey came rushing in. They took one look at me and FROZE with their mouths dangling open.

That's when Chloe grabbed a mildewy mop and brandished it at me menacingly. "WHO ARE YOU?

AND WHAT DID YOU DO WITH OUR FRIEND NIKKI?" she snarled.

"Listen, YOU! I have a dangerous weapon! And I'm NOT afraid to use it!" Zoey said, digging through her purse. "Wait! It's in here somewhere!"

Finally she pulled out her cell phone and pointed it right at me like it was loaded or something.

"DON'T MOVE!! Or I'll, um . . . SHOOT!!" she yelled.

I just rolled my eyes at my friends.

Apparently, Chloe was going to MOP me to death while Zoey recorded it on her cell phone.

Then WHAT were they going to do?!

Post it on YouTube?!

"Both of you! Just CALM down!" I said. "It's ME!"

"Sorry, but we don't know anyone named MIA!" Chloe said, narrowing her eyes at me. "Now, WHERE'S Nikki?!"

Okay, I'd had quite enough. I grabbed that mop from Chloe and resisted the urge to smack her with it.

"IT'S ME! NIKKI MAXWELL!"
I yelled.

Both Chloe and Zoey looked relieved. "NIKKI!"

Then Zoey gave me a puzzled frown. "If you don't mind me asking, WHY are you wearing a ski mask?"

I hesitated, trying to come up with a logical explanation.

But there was no intelligent way to say "I turned myself into a mutant blueberry because I wanted to look PRETTY."

So I decided to just stick with the facts. . . .

"WHAT?!!" Chloe and Zoey exclaimed. That's when I totally lost it!

"I'm BLUE!" I wailed. "You gotta help me!
I'm BLUE!!"

But my BFFs must have thought I had invited
them to the janitor's closet for a PITY PARTY
or something because I was feeling, um . . .
BLUE!

"Poor thing!" Chloe pouted. "Don't worry! We'll
cheer you up and put a smile back on your face!"

"Nikki is bery, bery SAD!" Zoey said in an annoying
baby voice. "I tink she needs a willy big hug!"

They both grabbed me and gave me a big bear hug.

"Now does Nikki feel better?" Zoey asked. "Because
we WUV you! We willy do!"

"You DON'T understand!" I said, snatching the ski
mask off my head. "SEE?!"

Chloe and Zoey just stared at me in shock for what
seemed like forever. Then they shrieked . . .

"Your FACE!" Zoey gasped. "It's like . . . cobalt blue! Sort of . . ."

"No, it's WAY worse." Chloe grimaced. "It's more like, um . . . toilet-bowl-cleaner blue! Or maybe . . ."

"SMURF BLUE!!" Chloe and Zoey said excitedly.

"Who CARES what shade of blue it is? I can't take my student ID photo like this!" I muttered, flushing red with embarrassment.

Which meant right then my face was probably a vibrant shade of purple.

Like, grape Popsicle purple!

I continued. "I can't get the color off! And now I have to wear a ski mask for the rest of my life! Do you know how HUMILIATING it will be to wear a ski mask to my WEDDING?" I ranted. "WELL, DO YOU?!"

"Nikki, just calm down!" Chloe said.

"I'm supposed to be getting my student ID photo for North Hampton Hills RIGHT NOW!

88

But I'm toilet-bowl blue and I look like an ALIEN CREATURE! And if I wear this stupid ski mask, I'll look like a BURGLAR. How am I supposed to go to Paris looking like THIS? TELL ME HOW!" I screamed.

"Girl, get a grip!" Zoey grabbed me by my shoulders to shake some sense into me. "Now explain how all of this happened."

"Yogurt," I muttered, blinking back tears.

"Wait a second! Did you just say 'YOGURT'?!" Chloe asked.

"Yes!" I sniffed. "I tried to make some fancy yogurt facial cream at home using Princess Sugar Plum blueberry yogurt and some other stuff. All I wanted was beautiful and radiant skin. But now I'm a blue . . . MONSTER!"

"Toilet-bowl-blue monster!" Zoey smirked. "But the good news is that it's just food dye, which is the same ingredient used in a lot of makeup.

Luckily, I have a mini pack of makeup remover wipes in my purse. So have a seat and watch me work my magic! Chloe, please assist. . . ."

CHLOE AND ZOEY CLEAN MY FACE!!

Within ten minutes my face was back to normal.
Almost! Due to my homemade facial cream, my skin
was now clear and silky smooth, with a radiant glow!

Chloe and Zoey were SO impressed, they begged to
try some of my facial cream too.

Then we rushed down to the library and made it
just in time to get our student ID photos. I think
mine came out SUPERcute! . . .

NORTH HAMPTON HILLS
INTERNATIONAL ACADEMY

NIKKI MAXWELL
Student Exchange Week

Maybe my homemade facial cream will make
me a BILLIONAIRE after all.

☺!!

Chloe and Zoey are the best friends EVER!

Thanks to them, not only did I look like a cover
model, but by lunchtime I had received a half
dozen compliments on my lip gloss, eye shadow,
and blush.

And I wasn't even wearing any!

As Chloe and Zoey dug into the huge mound
of chocolate pudding that was our lunch dessert,
I suddenly had a painfully nauseating flashback.

"EW! I'll NEVER, EVER eat that stuff again!!"
I muttered in disgust.

"Really, Nikki? So do you mind if I ask you a
question?" Chloe said.

"You want to know WHY I suddenly HATE

92

chocolate pudding, right?" I asked. "Well, it's kind of a long story. Brianna has been trying to earn a cooking badge. And earlier this week she made this AWFUL batch of pudding that looked like mud and—"

That's when Chloe interrupted me. "Actually, Nikki, I was going to ask you if I could EAT your chocolate pudding," she said as she reached over with her spoon and greedily gulped down the entire thing before I could answer.

"BUURRP! Oops! Excuse me!" Chloe giggled.

Did I ever mention that Chloe has the table manners of a barnyard animal?

Zoey folded her arms. "Now I'm REALLY curious. You stopped right in the middle, and I'm DYING to hear the rest of it."

"Okay, if you insist." Chloe grinned as she inhaled a deep breath. . . .

"Chloe, not YOU!" Zoey said, rolling her eyes. "I want to hear what happened with Brianna's cooking badge. Did she ever earn it?"

"No! Her burnt chocolate pudding was a DISASTER! And, unfortunately, she wants to try to cook ANOTHER snack for her NEXT meeting," I complained.

That's when Chloe and Zoey excitedly volunteered to come over to my house tomorrow to teach

Brianna how to make their specialty . . .

HAND-TOSSED PEPPERONI PIZZA!

I have to admit, Chloe and Zoey's pizzas are DELISH!!

Although I felt really bad for Brianna, I was more worried about a SECOND cooking disaster!

"Guys, I really appreciate you wanting to help my sister, but she can barely make a bowl of cereal. Pizza is going to be WAY too difficult for her!" I grumbled.

"Don't worry, Nikki," Zoey said. "Chloe and I will basically make the pizza FOR her!"

"That's right!" Chloe agreed. "The three of us will be right there supervising her. What could possibly go wrong?!"

EVERYTHING!!

☹!!

95

In spite of my BFFs' assurances, I still had a really bad feeling about Brianna the pizza chef.

Chloe and Zoey arrived this afternoon with the ingredients to make three pepperoni pizzas. One was for Chloe's family, one was for Zoey's family, and one was for Brianna.

Zoey's job was to make the dough, mine was to spread the tomato sauce on the dough, Chloe's was to place the pepperoni, and Brianna's was to sprinkle the mozzarella cheese on top. Everything was going fine until Brianna decided she wanted to do Zoey's job.

"Hey! I wanna throw that pizza dough up in the air just like Zoey!" Brianna squealed.

"No, Brianna!" I said, shooting her a dirty look.

Then she excitedly grabbed the dough. "Watch this! I'm gonna throw it really high!" . . .

96

BRIANNA TOSSES THE PIZZA DOUGH!!

"Brianna!" I yelled at her. "WHAT are you doing? Give that pizza dough back to Zoey right now, before you accidentally—"

BRIANNA MISSES THE PIZZA DOUGH!

OMG! I was so DISGUSTED!!

Brianna looked like the Pillsbury Doughboy's half-human little sister.

Our attempt to help her make a pizza had turned into a CATASTROPHE!

"Who turned out the LIGHTS?!" Brianna giggled.

Then she started staggering around the kitchen like a dough-covered ghost, yelling, "BOOO! BOOOO!" as if it were Halloween or something.

Chloe and Zoey couldn't help but crack up at my bratty little sister's CRAZY antics.

But this situation was NOT a joke!

Brianna had totally RUINED the snack she was preparing for her Scout meeting!

AGAIN!!

Chloe and Zoey each tried to give Brianna their pizza, but I wouldn't let them.

The pizzas they had made were supposed to be dinner for THEIR families.

"But HOW am I supposed to earn my cooking badge with no PIZZA?!" Brianna whined.

"Sorry, Brianna!" I said sternly. "But if you hadn't been GOOFING around, you would NOT be wearing your pizza dough right now! All of this is YOUR fault!"

So, unfortunately, Brianna didn't earn her cooking badge by making pizza.

But she definitely could have earned a new badge for . . .

☹!!

I barely slept last night, and by morning I was a nervous WRECK! I felt like a 105-pound bundle of jittery nerves in a chic North Hampton Hills school uniform.

I stood in front of my mirror, plastered a fake smile across my face, and practiced introducing myself to imaginary NHH students.

"Hi, I'm Nikki Maxwell, and I'm from Westchester Country Day Middle School!"

"Hi, I'm Nikki Maxwell, and I'm looking forward to my week here at North Hampton Hills!"

"Hi, I'm Nikki Maxwell, and right now I'm so gut-wrenchingly nervous, I need to find the nearest bathroom and THROW UP! Be right back!"

But when I set foot on the campus, I forgot my nervousness. I was totally blown away again by the pure AWESOMENESS of North Hampton Hills! . . .

OMG! It is the most FABULOUS school I've ever seen in my entire LIFE!

Manicured lawns and dozens of trees give it a peaceful, parklike atmosphere.

The interior of the school is even more impressive. The main entrance has a huge fountain that is even LARGER than the one at the mall. There are tall columns, arched hallways, shiny marble floors, elegant chandeliers, and a courtyard with a fishpond and a rose garden!

I feel like a traitor even thinking this, but NHH makes Westchester Country Day look like a basic, no-frills daycare center!

When I got to the office (which looks like the lobby of a luxury hotel), I filled out an exchange student registration form and handed my NHH student ID to the secretary.

"Good morning, and welcome to North Hampton Hills!" She smiled. "So, you're Nikki Maxwell? We have a new transfer student from your school. Do you know MacKenzie Hollister?"

"Um, actually, I do," I answered. "We had lockers right next to each other."

She glanced around the room to make sure no one was listening, leaned toward me, and then whispered, "Most of the kids here are wonderful. But there are a few you'll want to avoid. They can be a bit . . . snobbish."

"Thanks! But you don't have to worry," I assured her. "I've known MacKenzie for a long time, and I'm used to her drama. I'll be just fine."

The secretary blinked in surprise. "Actually, it's NOT MacKenzie I'm warning you about. She's such a nice, sweet girl! And friendly, too," she gushed, and turned back to her computer.

I just stared at that lady like she was crazy, because OBVIOUSLY we were NOT talking about the same person. Who would use the words "NICE," "SWEET," and "FRIENDLY" to describe MacKenzie Hollister, the most selfish, manipulative SHE-SNAKE in the world?!

It was quite apparent that this secretary was yet another of MacKenzie's many hapless victims. She had SLITHERED into this office and somehow BRAINWASHED this poor woman.

"Please have a seat, dear," the secretary said. "A student ambassador will be here any minute to give you a tour of the school. I hope you have a fun week!"

"Thank you," I said as I slowly backed away from her desk and sank into a large plush chair.

My nervous stomach was starting to make garbage disposal sounds again. I suddenly felt really queasy as a wave of despair rushed over me.

Maybe coming to North Hampton Hills was NOT such a good idea after all.

☹!!

I was still waiting in the school office when I
spotted a gorgeous girl with auburn hair, a red
designer purse, and matching stilettos.

She easily could've passed for MacKenzie's
darker-haired twin sister.

Since she was holding a sign that said WELCOME,
NIKKI!, I assumed she was my student ambassador
guide for the week.

I grabbed my bag, thanked the secretary, and walked
down the hall to meet her.

My heart pounded as I took a deep breath and
introduced myself just like I had practiced in my mirror.

Yes, I know!

I could NOT believe that I actually said all of that
EITHER. . . .

"Hi, I'm Nikki Maxwell, and I'm from Westchester Country Day Middle School. I'm looking forward to my week at North Hampton Hills. But right now I'm so gut-wrenchingly NERVOUS, I really need to find a bathroom and—!"

But I didn't get a chance to warn her I was about to THROW UP, because the girl dropped the welcome sign and practically TACKLED me! . . .

OMG! I'M SO HAPPY TO FINALLY MEET YOU, NIKKI! I'VE HEARD SO MUCH ABOUT YOU!

"My name is Tiffany Blaine Davenport, and I'll be your guide while you're here!" the girl squealed excitedly. "I have a feeling we're going to be BESTIES!"

"Um, it's nice to meet you, too, Tiffany!" I replied as I wondered exactly WHAT she had heard about me.

"Now that we've introduced ourselves, I think we should celebrate our new friendship." She giggled as she whipped out her cell phone. "IT'S SELFIE TIME!"

"Well, okay!" I said as I stood next to her and smiled for our picture.

Tiffany lowered her phone and looked at me like I was a huge zit that had just popped out on her FLAWLESS face.

"Um, SORRY! But there's no 'us' in the word 'SELF-IE'!" she quipped. "I'm so FIERCE that I need to take photos ALONE so there's enough space in the lens to capture ALL of MY exquisite beauty! Now, be a good BFF and get out of my way, PLEASE! By the way, I love your shoes!"

Then Tiffany gently shoved me aside in a really friendly manner.

How DARE that girl disrespect me like that! Especially after I'd only known her for, like, THREE minutes.

At least she was "nice" enough to let me participate in her supermodel-style selfie fashion shoot.

I got to stand off camera and vigorously fan her with my welcome sign to create the windblown hair effect.

Are we having fun yet?!

I couldn't help doing a giant eye roll.

While I stood there fanning Tiffany for what seemed like forever, I had a really BAD feeling (in addition to the intense cramping in my arms) that our so-called friendship was going to be a little unusual!

Tiffany wanted to be MY BFF ☺! But it appeared she wanted ME to be HER brainless zombie servant ☹!

Anyway, after we finally finished that awkward, spontaneous photo shoot, Tiffany helped me find my locker.

She introduced me to her BFFs, Hayley and Ava, who bragged nonstop about how the three of them were THE trendiest and most fashionable CCPs (Cute, Cool & Popular kids) at NHH, with a rep for throwing the wildest parties.

I couldn't help doing ANOTHER giant eye roll. Although they seemed to be SUPERimpressed with themselves, I wasn't at all.

Then Tiffany gave me a ninety-minute tour of the HUMONGOUS school. OMG! The place was so massive I could've ended up lost for days.

Once we finished the tour, we stopped by the office to pick up my class schedule. . . .

NORTH HAMPTON HILLS Class Schedule		
NIKKI MAXWELL		
Class	Time	Teacher
History	8:00–8:50 a.m.	Mr. Schmidt
Geometry	9:00–9:50 a.m.	Mrs. Grier
Biology	10:00–10:50 a.m.	Mr. Winter
French	11:00–11:50 a.m.	Madame Danielle
Lunch	12:00–12:50 p.m.	N/A
Physical Ed	1:00–1:50 p.m.	Ms. Chandran
Study Hall	2:00–2:50 p.m.	Mr. Park

MY CLASS SCHEDULE

I really appreciated that Tiffany wanted to give me some "invaluable advice along with the latest dirt" on all of my teachers and classes. BUT it was definitely NOT what I expected to hear from a student ambassador. . . .

TIFFANY'S ADVICE TO ME ABOUT MY NORTH HAMPTON HILLS CLASSES

HISTORY CLASS: "Mr. Schmidt is a senile old dude who loves ranting about when he attended NHH as a kid during the Stone Age. He's also blind as a bat and won't see a thing if you chill out in the back row and text your friends, polish your nails, or take a beauty nap. Not that I need a beauty nap. Although I think YOU could definitely use a few. No shade intended!"

GEOMETRY CLASS: "Mrs. Grier gives us pop quizzes once a week. But only a total loser would spend their weekends studying for them instead of hanging out and partying. I just copy answers from Hannah Stewart. She sits in front of me and always gets straight As. Just remember not to copy her NAME on your test. I did that once, and Mrs. Grier completely FLIPPED OUT and failed me! That lady is CRAZY!!"

BIOLOGY CLASS: "Mr. Winter's class is a breeze! Whenever he loses his lesson plan book (which happens a lot), instead of teaching he just shows us the same movie, *Jurassic Park*, which he says is a 'biting critique of the negative impact of unfettered cloning on modern civilization.' So far we've seen that movie eleven times. This MONTH! How does he keep losing his lesson plan book, you ask? It might have something to do with a SUPERsmart (and SUPERstylish) thief stealing it before class. You're welcome!"

PE CLASS: "This week we'll be going horseback riding on the trails. Get to the stable early to select your horse. Coco and Star are the friendliest and best behaved. WARNING! Avoid Buddy the Shetland pony. Despite his tiny size and cute name, he is NOT your buddy! That thing is a wild BEAST! Meet me at the stable ten minutes before class."

FRENCH CLASS: "Madame Danielle is the snobbiest and meanest teacher in the entire school. But right now she's also the most POPULAR because she's taking a group of students on an all-expenses-paid trip to Paris this summer. It's been like the Hunger Games around here, with kids fighting to the death for a spot. The most important thing to know about her is that she's secretly obsessed with sweets. If you want to get on her good side, just bribe her with a box of chocolate truffles. That's, like, the ONLY reason I'm not failing her class!"

Thanks to Tiffany, I found out that Madame Danielle is the head of the foreign languages department and the advisor for the trip to Paris.

I excitedly explained to Tiffany that my French teacher at WCD had recommended me for that program and that I was DYING to go to Paris!

I immediately rushed down to the office to request an appointment with Madame Danielle.

So now I'm scheduled to meet with her on Friday. SQUEEEEE ☺!!

Although, to be honest, she seems kind of mean. What if she HATES me?! Seriously, I'm already SCARED of her and I haven't even met her yet.

I'm just PRAYING she'll select ME to go to Paris.

It will be the BEST thing that has EVER happened
to me in my ENTIRE life! . . .

MONDAY—3:00 P.M.
AT MY NHH LOCKER

At lunchtime Tiffany invited me to sit at a table with her and seven of her closest friends.

The NHH cafeteria is set up like the food court at the mall, but bigger and with better-tasting gourmet choices.

Although I was trying my best to be friendly, Tiffany was starting to get on my LAST nerve. This girl was so VAIN that she took a selfie, like, every ten minutes.

Next she asked me to go get HER a lunch since I was getting MY lunch. Then she asked me to dump HER lunch tray since I was dumping MY tray. And finally she asked me to carry HER books since I was carrying MY books.

OMG!

I totally LOST IT!

I yelled at her in front of the ENTIRE cafeteria. . . .

ME, SCREAMING AT TIFFANY!!

But I just said that inside my head, so no one else heard it but me!

My first day here at North Hampton Hills has been very, um . . . EXHAUSTING!!

But unless I want to drop out of the student exchange program and give up all hope of going to Paris, I don't have any choice but to try to put up with Tiffany and her phony friends.

Hey, it's only for FOUR more days!

The GOOD NEWS is that things CAN'T get any WORSE!!

The BAD NEWS is that I might be really WRONG about the GOOD NEWS!

Why does attending North Hampton Hills feel like I'm living in some INSANELY FREAKY alternate universe?

This morning Tiffany, Hayley, and Ava met me at the front door. Tiffany greeted me with a big hug and air kisses. "So, how is my new BFF today? Love your shoes!"

Hayley and Ava just looked me up and down with contempt and didn't say a word.

Jealous much?!

As we walked down the hall, Tiffany was so busy texting her latest selfie that she accidentally slammed into a guy carrying a book bag, a small box, and what looked like a plastic lightsaber.

Stunned, he lay sprawled on the floor next to his glasses. . . .

TIFFANY ACCIDENTALLY BUMPS INTO
A STUDENT AND KNOCKS HIM OVER!

"You clumsy IDIOT!" Tiffany snarled. "How am I supposed to send a text with you body-slamming me like this is the Super Bowl?"

"I'm s-sorry, Tiffany!" the guy stammered, slightly dazed as he slowly picked himself up.

"You science club geeks are so PATHETIC!" Hayley scowled. "And aren't you a little old to be bringing your toys to school?"

"I bet it's for show-'n'-tell! Well, you better get going, because the second-grade classrooms are in the elementary school building down the road." Ava laughed as the guy hobbled away, humiliated. "Get a LIFE!"

Tiffany resumed texting, and said, "I can't wait for you guys to see the two selfies I took this morning of me brushing my teeth and eating my pancakes! You're going to LOVE them!"

I stood there in shock, pondering whether these girls were extremely CRUEL or just mind-numbingly CLUELESS!!

I finally decided they were BOTH! And it made me so ANGRY I wanted to . . . SPIT!!

"Actually, Tiffany, it looked to me like YOU bumped into that guy," I said, highly annoyed. "Thank goodness he wasn't hurt."

She suddenly stopped texting and stared at me. Hayley and Ava folded their arms and wrinkled their noses like I'd just sprayed myself with a new fragrance called Fresh Cat Pee.

"Nikki! What's YOUR problem? I think you're just JEALOUS of my FAB selfies," Tiffany said accusingly as Hayley and Ava nodded in agreement.

"I don't have a problem. But if you text in a crowded hallway, you're probably going to bump into people," I tried to explain patiently.

All three girls gave me such giant eye rolls, I thought their eyeballs were going to pop out and roll down the hall. . . .

ME

TIFFANY AND HER BFFS,
EYEBALLING ME ALL EVIL-LIKE

"So, you're going to PRETEND to be Miss Perfect!"
Tiffany smirked. "Sorry, Nikki! But everyone here
has heard about YOUR reputation!"

"I know I'm not perfect," I said, defending myself.
"But I don't go out of my way to be unusually
CRUEL to people either."

"Oh, really? Then why did that MacKenzie Hollister girl transfer to this school to get away from YOU?" Hayley asked.

"According to the latest gossip, you made her life totally MISERABLE!" Ava said.

"That's NOT true!" I exclaimed.

"Well, I'D be MISERABLE too if someone RUINED my big birthday bash by sabotaging the chocolate fountain so that my BFF and I ended up completely drenched in chocolate!" Tiffany sneered.

"Yeah, and you CHEATED in your school's ART show, you CHEATED in the TALENT show, and you CHEATED in the charity ICE show!" Hayley taunted.

"Not to mention the fact that you SHOVED that poor girl into a Dumpster during the Sweetheart Dance! And PUSHED her down a SKI SLOPE! She could have been KILLED!" Ava said scornfully.

"Sorry, but NONE of those things are true!" I shot back. "They're all just nasty rumors that someone is spreading about me. I would NEVER, EVER do ANY of those HORRIBLE things!"

"Okay! So you DIDN'T toilet-paper MacKenzie's house in the middle of the night with some of your CCP friends?!" Tiffany asked, narrowing her eyes at me.

Hayley and Ava stared at me too, with complete disdain.

Of course all this made me REALLY mad.

"NO. I. DIDN'T!!" I screamed.

Then an awful memory suddenly popped into my head and kind of freaked me out.

You know, the memory from five months ago of me having a sleepover at Zoey's and toilet-papering MacKenzie's house in the middle of the night on New Year's Eve!! . . .

ME AND MY BFFS TOILET-PAPER
MACKENZIE'S HOUSE

"Well, um . . . OKAY!" I muttered. "Now that I think
about it, maybe I DID pull a prank on MacKenzie
by toilet-papering her house. But I didn't do
ANY of the other scandalous stuff! So don't even
go there!"

"Just admit it, Nikki! You're a Queen Bee just like ME! You ruthlessly go after whatever you want and will totally annihilate anyone or anything that gets in your way. I actually ADMIRED that about you! Until you turned on me like a pack of wolves," Tiffany growled.

"This is INSANE! I just suggested that you NOT text in a crowded hallway! How is THAT turning on you?" I responded.

"Sorry, Nikki! But I UNFRIEND YOU! Come on, girls, let's go!" Tiffany exclaimed. "I need to capture this very intense moment in my life with another SELFIE!"

Then Tiffany, Hayley, and Ava sashayed down the hall. I just HATE it when snobby mean girls sashay!

I went straight to the luxurious east wing, to my oversize locker, near a beautiful, SUPERexpensive chandelier, and started writing about everything that had just happened. . . .

ME, WRITING IN MY DIARY

Even though I was in a HUGE school filled with hundreds of students, I suddenly felt all alone!

I swallowed the large lump in my throat as my eyes filled with tears ☹!

I NEVER thought I'd EVER miss my friends and my school, WCD, so much!

There was no doubt in my mind that Tiffany, Hayley, and Ava were definitely the mean girls that the office secretary had warned me about.

And the less I had to do with them, the better.

☹!!

My first four classes seemed to drag on FOREVER!

It didn't help that Tiffany was whispering about me and shooting me dirty looks.

It was like she hated me worse than knockoff designer purses.

Finally it was lunchtime. I grabbed a steak burger with waffle fries for lunch and yummy frozen yogurt with fresh strawberries for dessert.

Most of the kids in the cafeteria were sitting with their friends.

But since I didn't have any, I found an empty table in the very back near the garbage cans so I wouldn't bother anyone.

Then the strangest thing happened!! . . .

ME, SURPRISED THAT SOME GUYS
ASKED TO SIT AT MY TABLE

"I'm Patrick. And this is Lee, Drake, and Mario," he
said as they all took a seat.

"Hi, guys!" I smiled. "So, how did you know MY name?"

"EVERYONE knows your name!" Lee answered. "We've been hearing stuff about you for the past month! I guess you're famous at NHH!"

I took a bite of my hamburger and shrugged. "I almost hate to ask, but famous for WHAT?"

They looked at each other and then back at me. "Well, for your, um . . . reputation," Drake replied.

"That sounds more like INFAMOUS to me! If it's any of the rumors I heard this morning, NONE of them are true," I grumbled.

"THEY'RE NOT?!" the guys exclaimed, obviously disappointed.

"Actually, we were hoping they were," said Lee.

"Tiffany is on a power trip, and she runs this school like a prison warden. But we've heard she's really intimidated by you. We should form an alliance!" Mario said.

"An alliance? What kind of alliance?" I asked.

"Well, if you can help us, maybe we can help you!" Drake answered.

"Help you with what?" I asked, a bit suspicious.

"We're members of the science club. But to keep our funding we have to maintain a membership of at least six students in addition to our four-member executive board. Since we have less than that, we'll be losing our funding on Monday and won't be a club anymore," Patrick explained. "And now Tiffany has convinced our student council president to replace us with her new selfie photography club. She said it would better serve the school since twelve people have already signed up."

"Well, have you ever tried a membership drive?" I asked.

"Yes, we had one in April. It was very successful and actually doubled our membership!" Lee said.

"That's great news! So how many members do you have NOW?" I asked.

"We went from TWO to FOUR members! But we still need six more. We put a sign-up sheet in the boys' locker room," Drake bragged. "Do you have any idea how many guys pass through there? Like, hundreds!"

"Come on! WHAT ABOUT GIRLS?!!" I shrieked. "No wonder no GIRLS signed up."

"I guess we messed up really bad. So will you help us?" Patrick pleaded.

"PLEEEEEASE!!!" the four of them begged.

"I'm really sorry, guys! But I don't think there's really anything I can do. Have you thought about joining the selfie club? It might be fun." I shrugged.

"Well, why don't we consider taking more, um . . . DRASTIC measures?" Patrick suggested.

"What do you mean by 'drastic'?" I asked.

The only DRASTIC measure I wanted to take was to stage an intervention for Tiffany to cure her annoying SELFIE ADDICTION. . . .

TIFFANY GETS MEDICAL TREATMENT FOR HER SELFIE ADDICTION!

"Drastic, like . . . I don't know," Drake said. "Maybe you could steal her diary and blackmail her into dumping the selfie club?"

"You could slam her in the face with a dodgeball so hard she gets amnesia and forgets all about her new club?" Lee suggested.

"You could put a bug in her hair and post it on YouTube so she'll transfer to a new school out of sheer humiliation?" Mario suggested.

I was getting sick and tired of people repeating all those rumors. "I KNOW!" I yelled sarcastically. "WHY DON'T I JUST PUSH TIFFANY OFF A SKI SLOPE SO SHE'LL BREAK HER NOSE AND NEVER WANT TO TAKE ANOTHER SELFIE AGAIN?!"

The guys started cheering and high-fiving each other.

"PERFECT!!" Patrick shouted.

"BRILLIANT!!" Lee roared.

"AWESOME!!" Drake cheered.

"EXCELLENT!!" Mario yelled.

"Sorry, dudes! I was kidding! That was just SARCASM!" I grumbled.

"Well, can you at least come to our meeting after school on Friday?" Patrick pleaded.

"I don't think so. But what usually happens at these meetings?" I asked out of curiosity.

"Well, we start by suggesting a daily activity. Then we vote YES or NO and drop them in the ballot box. Then we open it and count the votes," Mario explained.

"So your club does cool stuff like conduct experiments, visit technology museums, and enter science fairs, right?" I asked.

"No! We usually just do reenactments of our favorite lightsaber fight scenes from the Star Wars movies. It's really fun and exciting!" Lee exclaimed.

So THAT explained why Patrick was carrying that small box and lightsaber this morning.

"I don't know, guys!" I sighed. "Just let me think about it, okay? Maybe we can meet here tomorrow during lunch to discuss it some more."

So that was our plan.

The guys thanked me and headed off to class feeling hopeful.

But deep down I already knew there wasn't much I could do to help them save their science club.

☹!!

I felt really bad for Patrick and all the guys in the science club.

Hey, I knew from personal experience what it was like to face the WRATH of Tiffany. I only have to deal with her for the rest of the WEEK. But those poor guys are stuck with her for the rest of the YEAR!

Tiffany is just a mean girl whose hobby is RUINING other people's lives.

And speaking of mean girls. . . .

I had a really good hunch WHO was spreading all those NASTY rumors about ME.

I glanced at the clock on the wall and grabbed my book bag to rush off to class.

Then I turned around, stopped dead in my tracks, and found myself face-to-face with . . .

MACKENZIE HOLLISTER,
STARING AT ME IN SHOCK AND HORROR!

MacKenzie looked like she had just seen a ghost! Then she was all up in my face like, um . . . my homemade FACIAL CREAM!

I was so mad at her that I could have SLAPPED her into tomorrow!

But I would NEVER do anything like that because I am a very peaceful and nonviolent person.

I'm also very ALLERGIC to BEATDOWNS!

When I last saw MacKenzie at the CupCakery on April 30, she was there with her new friends from NHH. But it was quite OBVIOUS she was pretending to be ME. It was like she had stolen and assumed MY life but had kept her OWN name.

MACKENZIE'S LIST OF LIES
(HOW SHE STOLE MY LIFE!)

MacKenzie said SHE:

1. Had a band called Actually, I'm Not Really Sure Yet

2. Had a record deal with Trevor Chase

3. Was crowned Sweetheart Princess at her Valentine's dance with Brandon as her date

4. Had an advice column in our school newspaper called "Miss Know-It-All"

5. Was a regular volunteer at Fuzzy Friends Animal Rescue Shelter

6. Ran a book drive for the school library

7. Won a cash prize for charity in an ice-skating event

And as if all of THIS wasn't deranged enough, MacKenzie had ALSO started a dozen rumors saying that I had done all of the CRUEL stuff to HER that SHE had actually done to ME!

Anyway, I pointed MY finger right back in HER face and shouted . . .

ME, STARING AT MACKENZIE
IN SHOCK AND HORROR!

Things suddenly got really, really tense.

"I wouldn't WANT your PATHETIC life, Nikki! Now, WHAT are you doing at MY school?!"

"I'm in the student exchange program. But I DREADED coming to North Hampton Hills because of YOU! I'm only here because I want the FREE trip to PARIS sponsored by this school! My teacher at WCD said I had a good chance. But I'm probably wasting my time, because I've heard that the trip advisor, Madame Danielle, is really mean unless you BRIBE her with chocolate!" I yelled.

"Well, just mind your business while you're here! I'm not going to let you ruin my life. You have no idea what I had to go through to get into this school!"

"MacKenzie, you have it SO easy! Everything is handed to you on a silver platter!"

"You're WRONG! I shouldn't even be at this school. I freaked out on the entrance exam and scored so low that my parents had to donate a ton of money to get me admitted. So, Nikki, you have no clue!"

I glared at MacKenzie.

And MacKenzie glared at me.

That's when we suddenly heard someone snicker, "OMG! What a DRAMAFEST! I wish I had a bucket of popcorn!"

MacKenzie and I both turned around and gasped!

TIFFANY was standing right behind us, FILMING us with her CELL PHONE!

She stopped filming and flipped her hair.

Then she stepped right in front of us and struck a GLAM pose.

MacKenzie and I both stared at her in disbelief as she made a duck face and took a quick selfie. . . .

TIFFANY TAKES A SELFIE
WITH MACKENZIE AND ME!

"Sorry, girls! But both of you came from that
TRASHY school Westchester Country Day! You'll
NEVER be good enough for North Hampton Hills!
And my video is all the proof I need. So don't

think for one minute you're going to come here and take over MY spot as QUEEN BEE! It's so NOT happening!"

MacKenzie and I stared at each other. There was no question that we'd pretty much HATED each other from the first day we met.

Then we BOTH stared at Tiffany, a selfie-addicted diva intent on DESTROYING both of our lives. She was probably the ONLY person we both HATED more than EACH OTHER!!

Tiffany looked at the photo and giggled. "I think our selfie came out SUPERcute! I can't wait for you to see it. I'll text copies to you both, okay? You're going to LOVE it! See you later! Oh, BTW, I ADORE your shoes!"

I was completely FLABBERGASTED!

In just a few hours Tiffany had gone from being my new BFF to my NOT-SO-FRIENDLY FRENEMY!

Like, WHO does THAT?!

It suddenly became very clear to me.

There was just NO WAY that I was going to SURVIVE this program.

☹!!

WEDNESDAY, MAY 14—7:45 A.M.
AT MY NHH LOCKER

Having to deal with MacKenzie is really BAD!

And having to deal with Tiffany is HORRIBLE!

But having to deal with BOTH MacKenzie and Tiffany at the same time is enough to make me . . .

SCREEEEEEEEAM ☹!!

I seriously considered telling my mom I needed to stay home from school the rest of the week because I was really SICK and TIRED!

SICK and TIRED of MacKenzie trying to STEAL my life.

SICK and TIRED of Tiffany trying to RUIN my life.

I'm not sure how much MORE of their DRAMA I can take!

And if I had a choice, I'd much rather have a COMPLETE MELTDOWN in the privacy of my bedroom than at North Hampton Hills in front of hundreds of students.

There were two girls at the locker next to mine, and I couldn't help but overhear their conversation.

"Anyway, Tiffany said we need to sign up for the selfie club right away so it'll replace the science club. Although, to be honest, I'd much rather be in the science club than fanning the hair of CCPs for their photos," grumbled a girl with a ponytail.

"I totally agree! I didn't even know we HAD a science club," said her friend.

I decided to introduce myself. "Hi, I'm Nikki Maxwell. I'm from Westchester Country Day, and I'm visiting here as an exchange student."

"Hi, I'm Sofia, and this is my BFF, Chase," said the girl with the ponytail. "Wait a minute! Aren't

YOU the Nikki who tried to close down Fuzzy Friends Animal Rescue Shelter?"

"And WHY do you HATE puppies?!" demanded Chase. "They're SO ADORABLE!"

I was like, JUST GREAT ☹!!

"Um, that wasn't ME! It was some other girl named Nikki," I lied. "She sounds like an AWFUL person. Personally, I LOVE puppies!"

Sofia and Chase nodded in agreement.

I continued. "I was just wondering if you guys were interested in joining the science club. They're having a membership meeting on Friday and will be planning exciting activities for next year. We need your ideas. It'll be fun!"

"And girls in science, technology, engineering, arts, and math are SUPERCOOL!" said Sofia.

"Right! S.T.E.A.M. rocks!" added Chase.

"GREAT! JUST WRITE DOWN YOUR IDEAS
AND BRING THEM TO THE MEETING!"

"I'll be hanging out with a few science club members
at lunch if you'd like to join us," I said.

"Okay!" Sofia and Chase smiled.

There was still a lot to be done, but maybe our plan to save the science club just might work.

Tiffany will have a HISSY FIT once she finds out that her selfie club is in jeopardy.

But I am SO over Miss Queen Bee and her shady girl squad of Wanna Bees.

I have three important goals: (1) avoid Tiffany and MacKenzie like highly contagious diseases, (2) help Patrick save the science club, and (3) convince Madame Danielle to give me that trip to Paris!

Then I am OUTTA HERE!

!

When I got to biology, Mr. Winter had "lost"
his lesson plan book again, which meant we'd be
watching *Jurassic Park*.

Finally, it occurred to me why he showed that
movie over and over again during class.

It was to DISTRACT his students! He needed them
to shut up and leave him alone so he could search the
Internet for a NEW TEACHING JOB at another
SCHOOL!

The poor guy looked SUPERstressed.

I suddenly felt really sorry for him.

Tiffany was at her desk talking to her friends, and
when she saw me she did the strangest thing.

She walked up to my desk and gave me a HUG that
seemed to last FOREVER.

"Nikki, I want to apologize for what happened yesterday," she said sweetly. "Things just got out of control. I didn't mean any of what I said, and you were right all along. So are we cool?"

I was shocked!

A CCP had NEVER apologized to me before!

MacKenzie would rather be buried alive in a polyester party dress from Walmart with knockoff designer shoes than EVER apologize to anyone.

This was almost too good to be true.

Maybe Tiffany wasn't as evil as I'd made her out to be.

I decided to give her ONE more chance. But I still didn't completely TRUST her.

"Hey, it's no big deal. We're cool." I smiled.

"YAY!" she exclaimed. "I've got my bestie back!"

Then she returned to her desk and started giggling and whispering to her friends.

The teacher was about to turn off the lights and start the movie when Tiffany raised her hand.

"Mr. Winter, I just wanted to let you know that I saw someone SWIPE your lesson plan book."

I was really surprised to hear THAT news!

Especially since Tiffany had already confessed to me that SHE had been stealing his lesson plan book all year.

Mr. Winter scowled and raised an eyebrow. "Well, thank you, Miss Davenport! And who might this THIEF be?"

I was shocked and appalled by the totally SCANDALOUS thing Tiffany did next.

She stood up, pointed right at me, and said . . .

TIFFANY, ACCUSING ME OF
STEALING THE TEACHER'S BOOK

I just stared at her in disbelief! I already knew
Tiffany was a mean and snobby selfie addict. But I
DIDN'T know that she was ALSO a pathological liar!

"Mr. Winter, th—that's NOT true!" I stammered.
"I didn't take your lesson plan book! And it's NOT
in my book bag! I'll show you. . . ."

The entire class gawked at me as I frantically
dumped the contents of my bag on my desk.

"See, Mr. Winter? It's NOT here in my—"

I stopped midsentence and blinked in confusion.

A large brown leather book that I had never
seen before in my life was lying on top of my
textbooks.

I shot a dirty look at Tiffany. She must have slipped
the teacher's lesson plan book into my book bag
during her apology hug.

That selfie-addicted SNAKE just shrugged and
smiled at me all innocentlike.

Mr. Winter quickly strode across the room and
snatched his book off my desk. . . .

ME, TOTALLY FREAKING OUT ABOUT
MY TEACHER'S BOOK!

"Miss Maxwell, we have a zero-tolerance policy for THEFT," he said firmly. "Just so you know, I WILL be speaking to Principal Winston about your despicable behavior!"

"But, Mr. Winter, you don't understand! I would NEVER—!"

"Save your EXCUSES for when you get back to Westchester Country Day!" he said coldly.

I just sat there, numb, with my heart pounding in my chest like a bass drum.

I could hear Tiffany and her friends snickering behind me.

I was beyond HUMILIATED!

I wanted to dig a really deep hole right there in the classroom, CRAWL into it, and DIE!!

☹!!

WEDNESDAY—2:10 P.M.
IN STUDY HALL

Although I was still a bit traumatized by Tiffany and all the drama in biology, I was looking forward to hanging out with the kids from the science club during lunch.

Sofia and Chase sat at our table and shared their list of creative ideas for the club.

They both fit right in and got along really well with the guys.

I suggested that the Friday meeting in the science lab be a membership drive and PARTY, complete with Queasy Cheesy pizza.

Everyone LOVED my idea!

We all agreed to place science club sign-up sheets all around the school and not just in the boys' locker room.

Lee and Mario volunteered to handle the pizza and soft drinks. Patrick and Sofia agreed to do decorations. Drake offered to be our deejay and suggested a science-themed playlist that included his favorite old-school song, "She Blinded Me with Science."

That's when Chase excitedly suggested that the party theme be "Blinded by Science!" and volunteered to make matching posters.

She also had a brilliant idea for cool party favors that we could get SUPERcheap from the dollar store.

I reminded everyone how important it was to invite friends and other students to our science club party! Well . . . um, science club meeting.

Our goal was to show that science could be fun and exciting as well as interesting.

Anyway, everyone was so fired up that we completely lost track of time.

By the time we finished planning our event, lunch was over and we had less than a minute to scramble to our next class.

I wasn't all that worried about being late until I realized it was PE.

Yesterday we'd spent the entire class discussing the basics of horseback riding and how to do it safely.

And today we were actually going to be RIDING.

That's when I suddenly remembered Tiffany's WARNING about the importance of getting to the horse stable ten minutes EARLY to select a horse.

JUST GREAT ☹! I took off running and prayed that I'd get there before it was too late.

I quickly got dressed in my riding outfit and rushed out to the stable to sign up for a horse.

But, unfortunately, only ONE was left. . . .

"BUDDY THE PONY?!"

I just stared at him in shock. He was the EVIL
horse . . . I mean, pony . . . that everyone was
afraid to ride.

"Look at that nasty, ugly BEAST!" Tiffany sneered from behind me. "I think poor little Buddy is absolutely TERRIFIED of you!"

I was so mad, STEAM was practically coming out of my ears. But there was also steam coming from another place . . . Buddy's backside! EWW ☹! OMG! The stench of his gas was AWFUL. That pony smelled like he'd eaten nineteen cans of baked beans and seven really dirty, stinky gym socks.

The entire class rode out of the stable to the trails, except for Buddy and me.

"Come on, Buddy! Let's go!" I groaned and tapped him with my feet.

Buddy gave me a dirty look and neighed loudly.

"Quit complaining!" I fumed.

He angrily stomped his foot and passed more gas. Then he dashed out of the stable and down the trail and turned into a wild bucking bronco. . . .

BUDDY TRIES TO KILL ME WHILE
I HOLD ON FOR DEAR LIFE!

Tiffany and Ava rudely pointed and laughed.

"Yee-haw! Ride 'em, cowgirl!" Ava yelled.

"Wow! This is the funniest rodeo CLOWN SHOW ever!" Tiffany giggled. "Nikki, you're a goofball!"

I could not believe those girls were making JOKES when I could have been seriously injured or even KILLED by that CRAZY horse. However, after ten minutes, Buddy must have exhausted all his negative energy, because he suddenly calmed down and trotted along the trail and back to the stable like a show horse.

Everyone, including my teacher, was impressed that I had tamed Buddy with my superior horsemanship skills. But Tiffany and Ava just glared at me and rolled their eyes.

When we got back to Buddy's stall, I fed him a carrot for his good behavior. Then he passed gas, smiled at me, grunted, and fell fast asleep.

My little pony was my best BUDDY ever! ☺!!

WEDNESDAY—5:15 P.M.
IN MY BEDROOM

Chloe and Zoey stopped by after school today to see how things were going for me at NHH.

At first I tried to lie and tell them how wonderful everything was. But I finally broke down and told them the truth. It was a disaster!

MacKenzie was spreading nasty rumors about me and had pretty much stolen my life! Tiffany had secretly recorded me ranting about the French teacher, which meant I was NEVER going to be awarded that trip to Paris! And Mr. Winter thought I had stolen his lesson plan book and was going to report me to Principal Winston!

"Listen, Nikki, do NOT go back to that school!" Zoey pleaded with me. "Why are you punishing yourself like this?!"

"OMG! That place sounds HORRIBLE!" Chloe gasped. "How can you stand it?!"

That's when I burst into tears. . . .

WAAAAAAAH!!

"Listen, guys, you're right! But I've made new friends there, and I really want to say good-bye to them instead of just disappearing off the face of the earth," I said, sniffling.

So we all agreed that Thursday was going to be my last day at NHH, even if it meant having to attend summer school. Although I felt relieved this dramafest would be over soon, I couldn't help but feel a little worried about my friends in the science club. ☹!!

I was so stressed out about everything that I barely got any sleep last night.

My goal was to survive my last day at NHH. Things couldn't possibly get any worse, right?!

WRONG! During breakfast I got a text from MacKenzie!

She asked me to meet her at the fountain right before study hall to discuss OUR Tiffany problem. I texted "???," but she didn't respond.

During lunch the science club members sat at my table and chatted excitedly about the event tomorrow.

They thanked me for everything I'd done and told me the club had a special award they planned to give to me at the party. Then everyone started cheering.

I didn't have a choice but to break the bad news. "Actually, TODAY is going to be my last day at NHH. And even though I won't be able to attend the science club party, I'm sure it's going to be a huge success!"

I totally didn't expect what happened next.

"Nikki, if YOU'RE not going to be there, then why should we even bother?!" Patrick muttered in disappointment.

"I agree!" said Sofia. "You talked all of us into doing this, and now you're BAILING on us!"

"That's NOT fair!" everyone complained at once.

I had to tell them about the drama with MacKenzie, Tiffany, and Mr. Winter and how I needed to leave before things got even worse.

"But you told us to stand up to Tiffany and not let her close down our science club. If you leave early, YOU'RE letting Tiffany WIN!" Patrick argued.

I had to admit he had a good point. But when I explained that I was stressed out and leaving early might possibly resolve my problems, everyone finally understood.

I was really disappointed by what they did next.

"We're voting to cancel the science club meeting and allow it to become the selfie club," Patrick muttered. "Write 'YES' or 'NO' on your ballot and put it in the box, please. Nikki, you can count them."

I was like, JUST GREAT ☹!! As I counted the ballots I got a huge lump in my throat. There were six votes, and all of them were "YES!" for canceling the meeting.

My friends had given up and Tiffany had WON!

The rest of the day seemed to drag on forever.

I decided I'd clean out my locker and turn in my student ID card AFTER I met MacKenzie at the fountain. . . .

The first thing I wanted to know was WHY she
had started all those nasty rumors about me. I was
shocked when she told me her horror story. . . .

Tiffany and her friends had mercilessly teased MacKenzie about that video with the bug in her hair. So she started hiding out in the bathroom to avoid them. . . .

Tiffany went out of her way to make MacKenzie's life absolutely miserable, and MacKenzie became a social outcast without a single friend. . . .

SORRY, MACKENZIE! BUT THAT EMPTY SEAT IS ESPECIALLY FOR MY PURSE.

MacKenzie said she felt invisible because it seemed like all the students at NHH ignored her. So every day at lunch she sat all alone. . . .

Until one day she overheard some kids talking about the *15 Minutes of Fame* talent TV show.

And when she mentioned that the famous producer, Trevor Chase, had come to WCD back in March and worked with her and the band Actually, I'm Not Really Sure Yet, the NHH students mistakenly assumed she was the leader of my band.

They were SUPERimpressed! And the more MacKenzie talked about MY life, the more attention she got, the more popular she became, and the more friends she made.

Until she got so carried away with her tangled web of lies that she'd all but assumed MY life!

And to keep NHH students from possibly finding out who I REALLY was, she'd started the nasty rumors about me to create even more confusion.

It was SURREAL!!

But suddenly MacKenzie and I were RUDELY interrupted!

By TIFFANY ☹!!

"Sorry, girls! But I need to take some selfies for my weekly fashion blog of the new makeup brand I'm wearing. The spot you're sitting in has the most flattering light in the entire school. SO GET LOST!" she exclaimed as she shoved us out of the way.

MacKenzie and I stood in front of the fountain, glaring at that girl. Tiffany stepped on top of our bench like it was a stage, took several photos of herself, and then frowned.

"Darn it! The sunlight is right over the fountain!" she complained as she climbed up on its ledge. "Now get out of my photo!"

"I have a better idea!" MacKenzie scoffed. "Why don't you go CHOKE on your cell phone!"

"Don't hate me because I'm beautiful!" Tiffany sneered as she teetered on the edge of the fountain in her heels, striking various poses.

MacKenzie and I exchanged glances. I think we both had the same wicked wish.

Suddenly Tiffany's foot slipped and she lost her balance. "WHOA!!" she gasped loudly.

MacKenzie and I just stared in disbelief as she wobbled back and forth and back and forth in slow motion, wildly flapping her arms like she was a baby bird trying to fly for the first time.

Just as Tiffany was about to topple into the fountain, she grabbed MacKenzie's right arm in an attempt to regain her balance. Which worked for only about two seconds. Because Tiffany then knocked MacKenzie off balance, and the two of them teetered over the edge of the fountain together.

That's when I vaulted onto the ledge and grabbed MacKenzie's left arm and pulled her in the opposite direction like she was the rope in a game of tug-of-war.

Now all THREE of us were teetering back and forth over the edge of the fountain like some kind of weird circus act, trying not to fall in.

It was only after I grabbed MacKenzie's waist and pulled with all my might that the three of us finally tumbled into a big heap on the marble floor next to the fountain. Hey, at least we weren't IN the fountain!

But somehow the force of us falling had launched Tiffany's cell phone into the air.

She watched in HORROR as it fell into the fountain with a big SPLASH and quickly sank to the bottom!

"OH NO! MY PHONE!! MY PHONE!!" she screamed hysterically. Then she DOVE right into the fountain after it!

Soon Tiffany's shrieks echoed through the halls of the school. "OMG! MY CELL PHONE IS RUINED! HOW AM I SUPPOSED TO TAKE A SELFIE WITHOUT MY PHONE?!!"

That's when I whispered to MacKenzie, "Since Tiffany's phone is all wet, I really think we should be nice and help her out!" . . .

MACKENZIE AND ME, TAKING VIDEOS OF
TIFFANY FOR HER FASHION BLOG ☺!!

Tiffany continued her rant. "MacKenzie and Nikki, I HATE both of you!! I know you did this to get even with me. For stealing Mr. Winter's lesson plan book and blaming Nikki! For pulling all those mean pranks on MacKenzie and making her life MISERABLE! And for trying to shut down that STUPID and WORTHLESS science club so we can have my FABULOUS new selfie club! It's all YOUR fault I RUINED my precious phone! I promise you, I'm going to get even! So you both better watch your backs! Because I HATE YOU! I HATE YOU! I HATE YOOOOU!!"

Tiffany angrily stomped her foot, splashing water everywhere.

Then she accidentally dropped her phone AGAIN and dove back into the water to find it.

OMG! Tiffany's video was even more CRAY-CRAY than MacKenzie's wacky bug video!

MacKenzie and I smiled at each other. And then in a surprising and unprecedented show of unity, we actually did the unthinkable. . . .

WAY TO GO!!

MACKENZIE AND ME, GIVING EACH OTHER A HIGH FIVE!!

Tiffany was a selfie-addicted TYRANT! And hopefully just the fact that we had that video would make her think twice about retaliating.

Someone tapped me on my shoulder, and when I turned around, I was surprised to see Patrick standing behind me.

"WOW! Not only are Tiffany and her cell phone SOAKING WET, but it looks like her selfie club might be ALL WASHED UP too. Thanks to you!" He grinned.

"But my rep is ruined! Now there will be another nasty rumor that I'm so cruel I actually DROWNED a cell phone! So be afraid! Be VERY afraid!" I laughed.

"Well, I didn't want you to leave until I apologized for how everyone acted at lunch today. We were just disappointed that you weren't going to attend our meeting. We really appreciate you sticking up for us and helping to save our club. But things didn't work out like we'd planned," Patrick explained.

"No problem. Apology accepted. But, dude! It's about time you guys stopped playing with your lightsabers during meetings," I teased. "We're throwing that science club membership party tomorrow! And it's going to be a BLAST! So go round up the crew, and let's do this thing!"

☺!!

Today was my LAST day here at NHH, and my
schedule was jam-packed.

Tiffany didn't say a single word to me all day. I'm
guessing it's because I have a video of her confessing
and having a meltdown in the school fountain. Even
though her makeup was flawless, I'm pretty sure she
doesn't want to put MY video on her fashion blog ☺!!

I think MacKenzie and I are now FRENEMIES!
Which is a slight improvement over MORTAL
ENEMIES who HATE each other's GUTS. But hey,
at least it's progress!

Since Patrick and the rest of the crew are my
friends, I decided that helping them save their
science club was crucial.

We had agreed to meet at school an hour early
to post sign-up sheets and put up posters to help
generate excitement about joining our club.

I met Chase in the art room and was really
impressed with her posters. . . .

CHASE, YOUR POSTERS ARE AWESOME!

I was happy to see that our cool posters were getting a lot of attention in the halls.

My appointment to meet with Madame Danielle about the Paris trip was at noon, and I was a nervous wreck.

She started off by saying how much she'd enjoyed having me in her French class and that she'd heard a lot about me from other teachers, especially Mr. Winter.

I shuddered and braced myself for the news that I had been disqualified for the trip.

She said that Patrick and Sofia had met with Mr. Winter to explain that I hadn't stolen his lesson plan book and that, if anything, I would have immediately returned it to him.

He actually believed them since his book had been getting stolen for months before I'd arrived. So now Mr. Winter is recommending me for the trip, along with my French teacher from WCD!

Surprisingly, the meeting went really well. . . .

MADAME DANIELLE SAID SHE'D INFORM
STUDENTS OF HER DECISION ABOUT
THE TRIP TO PARIS IN THREE WEEKS!

She also explained that because of my art skills, she felt I would get even more out of the visit to the Louvre than most students.

So right now I'm really happy! In spite of my DISASTROUS week, I think I STILL have a really good chance of being awarded that trip to Paris!

SQUEEEEEE ☺!!

When the final bell rang, I rushed down to the science lab. The room was decorated with brightly colored balloons and the science club banner.

We had a table piled with food, and our music was blasting.

Although we were SUPERnervous, everything was finally ready.

I breathed a sigh of relief when we opened the classroom door and a long line of excited kids rushed inside. . . .

ME

Our science club membership drive party was a huge success!! Everyone LOVED our party favors! They were SUPERcool sunglasses that students got to keep.

And the cupcakes I had ordered from the CupCakery were absolutely DELISH!

Our ZANY music was lots of fun. And whenever our theme song, "She Blinded Me with Science," played, the entire room went NUTS!

OMG! Chase was such a great dancer. Sofia said she danced competitively and had won a ton of trophies.

We ended up with sixteen new members, for a total of twenty-two members! And, to show their appreciation, they gave me an honorary membership in the club! SQUEEEE ☺!!

When it was time to discuss club activities for next year, I couldn't help but make a joke. "Okay, all in favor of lightsaber fight scene reenactments from Star Wars movies, raise your right hand!" I said, all seriouslike.

Of course the only people to raise their hands were Patrick, Drake, Lee, and Mario.

"Okay! Now take your right hand and SLAP YOURSELF SILLY!" I joked.

Everybody in the room laughed really hard, including them. I think the guys got my point.

Soon it was time to say my good-byes, and we all hugged each other and agreed to stay in touch.

My week at North Hampton Hills had turned out better than I had imagined. But I was starting to worry that Tiffany's problem was possibly CONTAGIOUS. Why?

Because it was MY idea to take a CELEBRATORY SELFIE of me and the twenty-two members of the new-and-improved science club! I NEVER wanted to forget the wonderful time we had together being blinded by science!

OMG! I can't believe I actually SURVIVED the student exchange program at North Hampton Hills International Academy!

SQUEEEEEEEE ☺!!

Even though the science club event was a huge success, my last few minutes at NHH turned into a complete DRAMAFEST! I had just finished cleaning out my locker and was on my way to the office to turn in my student ID when I noticed a large group of kids crowded around a locker in the west hall.

Since NHH's soccer team was playing in a tournament, quite a number of students had stayed after school for the game. Curious, I rushed down the hall to find out what was going on.

OMG, I immediately had a disgustingly freaky case of déjà vu. . . .

SOMEONE HAD VANDALIZED
A LOCKER WITH GRAFFITI!

The shocking thing was that those exact same words had been written on my WCD locker back in October.

My dad is a bug exterminator and works for my school, Westchester Country Day. He also arranged for me to attend there on a full scholarship.

Unfortunately, MacKenzie found out about my deep, dark secret and started taunting me.

So when someone scribbled BUG GIRL on MY locker in red lip gloss, MacKenzie was my FIRST and ONLY suspect.

But WHY would someone write "BUG GIRL" on a student's locker at NHH?

Once the distraught owner of the locker showed up, the crowd quickly scattered.

That's when the entire fiasco finally started to make sense. I was stunned to discover that the locker belonged to . . .

MACKENZIE, FREAKING OUT ABOUT
THE GRAFFITI ON HER LOCKER!

I immediately suspected Tiffany since she had WARNED us to "watch our backs" in her angry rant yesterday. And MacKenzie had admitted that Tiffany had teased her about that video with the BUG in her hair when she'd started attending NHH.

I felt SUPERsorry for MacKenzie since she was obviously very upset. But I also couldn't help but wonder if she remembered vandalizing MY locker and writing those same cruel words.

MacKenzie was finally getting a taste of her OWN medicine, and she totally deserved it.

However, her spiteful actions had also made me feel hurt and alone. That's when I decided to be her friend, not her frenemy.

"MacKenzie, are you okay? This is such a cruel and disgusting prank!" I said. "I'm sorry you had to go through this!"

MacKenzie slowly turned around to face me, with tears streaming down her cheeks. . . .

200

MACKENZIE, ACCUSING ME OF
VANDALIZING HER LOCKER!

"Listen, MacKenzie!" I exclaimed. "I know you're angry right now. But I would NEVER stoop this low to hurt you or anyone else!"

"I don't believe you for one second! I think you came to NHH just to humiliate me!" MacKenzie screamed.

No matter how hard I tried to convince her that I was innocent, she refused to believe me.

Suddenly Tiffany appeared out of thin air.

"Hey, Nikki and MacKenzie, is something wrong? You two don't sound like BFFs anymore. OMG, MacKenzie! Did someone vandalize your locker? I wonder who HATES you that much?" she asked, batting her eyes all innocentlike. "Well, I'd love to hang out with you, but I gotta get back to that soccer tournament. Have fun!"

I definitely have to give Tiffany credit for being an evil genius. She'd probably heard one of the crazy rumors about how I'D vandalized MacKenzie's locker by writing "BUG GIRL" on it.

And actually doing the same thing to MacKenzie's NHH locker was the PERFECT setup!

Tiffany had effectively gotten even with MacKenzie and me by secretly launching World War III!!

Our new "friendship" had barely lasted twenty-four hours. And, ironically, now BOTH of us had been ridiculed as BUG GIRLS.

I just sighed and walked away.

Turning in my NHH student ID to the office was kind of bittersweet because I was already starting to miss my new friends.

But it also meant returning to my wonderful life at WCD and hanging out with cherished friends who adored me.

And OMG! I can hardly wait to get back there!

☺!!

I was so physically and mentally exhausted from my week at NHH, I could have slept FOREVER!

I FINALLY dragged myself out of bed around noon, only because I had promised Brianna that I'd spend the afternoon in the kitchen helping her try to earn her cooking badge.

AGAIN ☹!!

I was eating lunch and skimming my mom's recipe book for quick and easy snacks when I got a text from Brandon:

BRANDON: So, how was your week at Hogwarts? Luv the tacky uniforms (LOL)!

NIKKI: It was good. Can't wait to get back to WCD. How was South Ridge?

BRANDON: We had fun hanging out with Max C. Definitely one cool dude. His lil' bro, Oliver, and Brianna are BFFs?

NIKKI: Yep! I'm trying to help her earn a cooking badge for Scouts. Any ideas for a super-EZ brat-proof snack?

BRANDON: How about caramel popcorn balls? Yummy too!

NIKKI: Popcorn balls?! Are you kidding me? Sounds way too complicated!

BRANDON: Nope. Super EZ! Even I can make them and I'm a cruddy cook. I made some last night.

NIKKI: Really?! What are the ingredients?

BRANDON: Just popcorn and caramel candy. Cooks in microwave.

NIKKI: That's all?! Very cool! Be right back . . .

NIKKI: We have popcorn ☺! But no caramel candy ☹!

BRANDON: I have a bag of candy. Will bring it right over.

NIKKI: You're coming to my house? NOW?!!

NIKKI: Brandon?

NIKKI: Hello? R U there?!

NIKKI: We'll just cook a PB & J sandwich!

NIKKI: ?????? ☹!!

I was a little worried when Brandon disappeared like that right in the middle of us texting each other.

About fifteen minutes later there was a knock on my front door. And when I opened it, Brandon was standing there holding a bag of caramels.

"You said you needed caramels, right?" He grinned. "And since I'm here, I'll share my secret recipe for popcorn balls and help out."

Brandon said his SUPEReasy recipe was only three steps: (1) melt twenty-eight caramel candies into a sauce with two tablespoons of water in the microwave, (2) cook one bag of popcorn, and (3) stir them together, shape into balls, and EAT!

He said it was an ingenious, foolproof recipe that he could make with his eyes closed. But was it Brianna-proof?

Brianna was excited about making popcorn balls! And Brandon and I were excited to be hanging out with each other after a long week apart. However, after Brandon prepared the sauce, Brianna got an attitude and started trying to boss everyone around. . . .

BRANDON AND ME, HELPING BRIANNA
MAKE POPCORN BALLS!

"Listen, Brianna, while Brandon stirs the caramel sauce, YOU get to microwave the popcorn. Doesn't that sound like FUN?!" I said cheerfully.

"NO! I WANNA STIR THE CARAMEL SAUCE!" She pouted.

"You're REALLY good at making popcorn. So that's going to be YOUR job," I said sternly.

I read the microwave popcorn box aloud. "Place ONE bag of popcorn in microwave. Set microwave to cook for FOUR minutes. Makes THREE servings."

"Okay, I'll make the STUPID popcorn!" Brianna finally muttered. "But as soon as I'm done, I'm gonna STIR the caramel sauce and TASTE it too! You're NOT the boss of ME!"

Then she stuck her tongue out at me. I was SUPERembarrassed that she was acting like such a BRAT in front of Brandon.

I handed Brianna the box of popcorn. "If you need any help, let me know."

Soon the caramel sauce was ready and cooling to room temperature and the popcorn was popping in the microwave. The sweet and savory aromas in the kitchen smelled delish!

Cooking with Brandon was actually kind of, um . . . ROMANTIC! SQUEEEEEEEE ☺!!

He stared at me and smiled, and I stared at him and smiled. All of this staring and smiling went on, like, FOREVER!

Until we were RUDELY interrupted by Brianna. She was gleefully stirring the caramel sauce and humming to herself. Suddenly she decided to sneak a taste and brought the huge bowl up to her mouth and tipped it sideways.

"Brianna! WHAT are you doing?!" I gasped. "Put that down right NOW before you accidentally—"

That's when Brianna said, "OOPS!!"

Brandon and I stared in horror as . . . SPLOOOSH!
The caramel sauce slowly poured down the front of her
shirt until she was covered in a huge, sticky MESS!

BRIANNA, IN A STICKY SITUATION

JUST GREAT ☹!! I grabbed some paper towels and was about to clean her up when I heard a ridiculously loud racket coming from the microwave.

POP-POP! POP-POP-POP! POP! POP! POP-POP! POP-POP-POP! POP-POP! POP! POP-POP! POP! POP! POP-POP! POP-POP-POP!

"Why does it sound like July Fourth fireworks in there?" I asked, peering inside the microwave and noticing it was completely filled with popcorn. "Brianna, WHAT did you do?!!"

"I did exactly what YOU said. I put in FOUR bags for THREE minutes to make ONE serving!" she yelled at me.

"NOOO!! The directions said ONE bag for FOUR minutes to make THREE servings!" I groaned.

"OOPS!!" Brianna muttered again.

I hit the stop button and opened the door to the microwave. I was shocked and surprised when . . .

BRIANNA AND I ARE PRACTICALLY BURIED
ALIVE IN A HUGE AVALANCHE OF POPCORN!!

What a DISASTER! It took us an hour to clean up
the humongous MESS Brianna had made.

She DID try to help! But because she was still covered in sticky caramel, she just ended up a giant ball of popcorn and random kitchen stuff! . . .

BRIANNA, THE HUMAN POPCORN BALL!

But at least she was a SUPERyummy human popcorn ball. . . .

BRIANNA SNACKS ON HERSELF!

Lucky for Brianna, Brandon had managed to save a cup of caramel sauce that was left over in the bowl, and I found a lot of popcorn still inside the microwave.

So Brianna was able to make a dozen mini popcorn balls, which she took to her Scout meeting later in the afternoon! . . .

BRIANNA'S MINI POPCORN BALLS

When Brianna got home, she excitedly explained how EVERYONE at her meeting LOVED her bite-size popcorn balls and begged for MORE!

Then she showed me her brand-new cooking badge! . . .

BRIANNA'S NEW COOKING BADGE

I congratulated my little sister and told her how proud I was of her that she had NOT given up.

Then I gave her a really big hug.

I was also proud of myself for being a mature, supportive, and patient big sister ☺!

UNTIL Brianna asked me to help her earn a gourmet chef badge. All she had to do was plan, prepare, and serve a formal four-course gourmet dinner for six people.

That's when I ran upstairs SCREAMING, locked myself in my bedroom, and hid in the back of my closet.

Sorry, but cooking with Brianna was a risky and dangerous activity, and, seriously, I would NEVER, EVER do it AGAIN ☹!!

Unless, of course, BRANDON was going to be Brianna's assistant chef!

SQUEEEEEE!!
☺!!!

OMG! I was SO happy to be back at WCD!
I wanted to KISS everything HELLO!

Like the walls, the floors, my locker, my textbooks,
and my very cute CRUSH, Brandon!

SQUEEEEEEE ☺!

Everyone shared exciting stories about the
schools they'd attended and the new friends
they'd made.

Like Brandon, Chloe and Zoey had enjoyed
attending South Ridge Middle School and hanging
out with Max C.

Of course I bragged about throwing a HUGE party
for my twenty-two new friends at NHH and showed
off the photos of the science club meeting.

Everyone was pretty impressed that I was such a
social butterfly.

Anyway, my day was PERFECT! Until I got a very
strange and ominous-sounding e-mail from Principal
Winston:

Monday, May 19

TO: Nikki Maxwell
FROM: Principal Winston
RE: MacKenzie Hollister

Dear Nikki Maxwell,

This is to notify you that MacKenzie Hollister has
requested an emergency meeting in my office
on Tuesday, May 20, at 10:00 a.m. concerning a
personal matter that involves you.

Please be prompt.

Thank you,
Principal Winston

JUST GREAT ☹!!

On Friday it was quite obvious that MacKenzie and Tiffany were still at war with each other.

But HOW did that involve ME at MY school?

I thought all the NHH drama had been resolved.

That's when I suddenly remembered MacKenzie's last day at WCD about a month ago.

She had threatened to file a phony complaint against me for cyberbullying her.

Only WHY would she do that NOW?!

I didn't know the answer, and it didn't really matter.

I was about to face my worst nightmare.

☹!!

TUESDAY, MAY 20—NOON
AT MY LOCKER

Today was my meeting with Principal Winston and MacKenzie, and I was a nervous wreck ☹!

"So, this is what I get for helping that drama queen get a bug out of her hair?" I fumed as I walked down to the office. "NEVER AGAIN!"

Back in April, one of MacKenzie's frenemies had secretly recorded her having a MELTDOWN about the bug in her hair and then texted the video to a few friends.

The video got circulated around the entire school, and one day during lunch MacKenzie caught her CCP friends watching it and laughing behind her back.

MacKenzie was so angry and humiliated, she stopped being friends with her BFF, Jessica, and demanded that her parents let her transfer to a new school.

When they refused, MacKenzie decided to take matters into her own hands. She secretly posted a copy of her own bug video on YouTube. . . .

MACKENZIE POSTS
HER BUG VIDEO ONLINE!

MacKenzie LIED and told her parents that the situation had escalated into a more serious one because Nikki Maxwell (ME?!) had posted the video online and was cyberbullying her.

Then she pleaded with her parents to transfer her to North Hampton Hills International Academy!

After her FAKE meltdown, complete with hysterical crying worthy of an Academy Award, her concerned parents relented and agreed to send her to a new school.

It's sad, but true! MacKenzie Hollister is such a cruel and malicious person that she had heartlessly cyberbullied HERSELF!

Anyway, when I arrived at the office for our meeting this morning, MacKenzie was already there, applying her lip gloss. The secretary was on her lunch break, and Principal Winston's door was closed.

"Hi, MacKenzie!" I said awkwardly.

She glared at me like I was something large, green, and slimy that she'd just sneezed into a tissue.

I decided to try to reason with her one last time.

"Why are you doing this, MacKenzie?! It makes no sense at all!"

"Actually, I have TWO very good reasons! First, if you're expelled for cyberbullying, then everyone at NHH will believe that I was telling the truth and YOU were lying. Second, Tiffany now HATES you as much as I do, especially since you undermined her beloved selfie club. Once I've FINALLY gotten even with you, she'll totally ADORE me and we'll become BFFs!"

"You'd actually TRUST Tiffany to be your BFF?!"

"Of course NOT! I'll just PRETEND to be her BFF . . . until I stab her in the back, label her an uncool, selfie-addicted weirdo, turn all her friends against her, AND steal her title as QUEEN BEE! It's all part of my carefully crafted master plan!"

"So, let me get this straight, MacKenzie. You'd LIE about me and completely DESTROY my life just to hang out with a popular girl at NHH?!"

"ABSOLUTELY! But don't take it personally, hon! I realize all of this is probably MY fault. But you have no idea how STRESSFUL and HUMILIATING it was to have that huge, icky BUG stuck in my hair."

It was quite obvious that this girl was out of touch with reality AND more SELF-ABSORBED than a SPONGE the size of New Jersey!

"Sorry, MacKenzie! But as someone who's been a real victim of cyberbullying—thanks to YOU, by the way—I have some invaluable advice for you. GET OVER IT!!!"

"I will. As soon as you're EXPELLED!!" She sneered. "All I have to do is convince that clueless slob, Principal Winston, that you're guilty. He'll believe anything I say!"

I watched in disbelief as MacKenzie took a mirror out of her purse and actually practiced her CRY FACE!

"Principal Winston!" she fake sobbed. "Nikki's bullied me, and it's been horrible! I saw her post that video with my own eyes! Please HELP me!! . . ."

MACKENZIE, PRACTICING FAKE CRYING

"And YOU'RE a pathological LIAR!" I shot back.

"You say that like it's a BAD thing!" She grinned.

Suddenly the office door opened and a lady wearing trendy, cute clothes entered with a cameraman in tow.

MacKenzie and I exchanged curious looks.

"What did you do, MacKenzie?! Contact a national NEWS network?!" I complained.

"No! I didn't," she replied. "I have no idea what they're here for."

"Excuse me! Do you girls have a minute?" the reporter asked. "We're with TeenTV News!"

"TeenTV?!" MacKenzie shrieked. "Are you going to be filming here at the school? If so, I need to put on my high-definition lip gloss!"

"Well, that depends," the reporter answered. "We're here to find out more about a video that was posted online on April 21. It was about a girl with a bug stuck in her—"

"OMG, Nikki! You sent that humiliating bug video to TeenTV?!" MacKenzie shrieked. "Why are you trying to RUIN my life?! I'll just lock myself inside the office supply closet until they leave."

Then she very rudely SHOVED me toward the reporter.

"Interview HER. It's ALL her fault. But be careful. She's so UGLY she might BREAK your camera!" MacKenzie sneered.

"SHOVE me like that again, girlfriend, and you'll see just how UGLY I can get!" I fumed.

But I just said that inside my head, so no one else heard it but me.

Since the school secretary was still at lunch, Mr. Winston was in his office, and MacKenzie had pretty much barricaded herself inside the office supply closet, I sighed and reluctantly agreed to talk to the reporter.

"We're looking for a student named Nikki Maxwell," the reporter said. "Do you know her? When we called here yesterday, we were given her name by a student office assistant named Jessica."

"Actually, she is ME! I mean, me is HER! What I'm trying to say is, I'M Nikki Maxwell," I babbled incoherently.

"Fabulous!" she replied. "Ready to film, Steve!" she cued her cameraman. "This is Jade Santana, coming to you live with a *TeenTV News* exclusive!"

Even though I was on television a few months ago (it's a long story and another diary!), I fidgeted uncomfortably and smiled awkwardly into the camera.

I had to restrain myself from grabbing the nearest wastebasket, shoving it over my head, and running out of the office SCREAMING!

The reporter continued. "I'm here with Nikki Maxwell, the mastermind and creator of the VIRAL video that is sweeping TeenTV and the nation . . . the STINK BUG SHAKE!" Jade exclaimed. "Congratulations, Nikki! You've just been nominated for the TeenTV Awesome Awards Best Viral Video of the Year!! How do you feel?"

That's when the office supply closet door slowly opened.

A very shocked and surprised MacKenzie cautiously peeked out.

"How do I feel? Um . . . REALLY confused!" I muttered. "Can you run all of that by me again, please? I'm not sure I understood everything you just said!"

"Well, Nikki, the teens of the world have spoken. And they LOVE your video!" Jade exclaimed. "Did you have any idea it was going to go viral?"

ME, BEING INTERVIEWED BY TEENTV FOR
BEST VIRAL VIDEO OF THE YEAR!!

Suddenly my interview with Jade was RUDELY interrupted.

"STOP! You should be interviewing ME, not HER!!" MacKenzie screeched as she jumped in front of me. "I'M the REAL STAR of that video!"

Then she got really close to the camera and did a DUCK FACE. That girl was a hot mess!

"Sorry! But WHO are you again?" Jade frowned.

"MACKENZIE HOLLISTER! I'M the one who posted that viral video of—what did you call it—the Stink Bug Shake that's sweeping the nation! NOT this pathetic POSEUR!" she said, pointing at me.

"Wait a minute, MacKenzie! For the past month, you've been spreading nasty rumors and telling EVERYONE that I posted that bug video!" I exclaimed. "So NOW you're CHANGING your story?!"

"Nikki, do you actually think I'M going to STUPIDLY stand by and let YOU take credit for all of MY

233

hard work?!" MacKenzie shrieked. "GIRL, BYE!"

Jade and the cameraman exchanged puzzled glances.
"Listen, girls, you're going to have to figure all of
this out and do it quickly. We're going live to finish
this segment in sixty, no, fifty seconds!" Jade said,
looking at her watch.

I couldn't believe I FINALLY had a chance to END
this NIGHTMARE once and for all.

"So, let me get this straight, MacKenzie! You're
willing to admit on national television that YOU
purposely put that video online and I had absolutely
nothing to do with it?" I asked.

"YES! You got it straight!" she snarled. "Just admit
it! You WISH you had BUGS in your hair like I do.
This is MY moment! Quit trying to steal it, you
basic, no-talent WANNABE!"

"Hello, I'm Jade, and we're back live for TeenTV!
So, MacKenzie, tell us how you first came up with
the concept for your fabulous video?" . . .

MACKENZIE, BEING INTERVIEWED BY
TEENTV ABOUT HER VIRAL VIDEO!

"When you're a trained dance GENIUS like I am, it all comes naturally! One day I was cleaning the girls' locker room showers when an idea just, um . . . crawled into my head. And then later, in class, it tangled itself in my hair and, um . . . became inspiration. It actually made me cry. Tears of joy! And then, to express the emotional rawness I was feeling, I started to scream! And jump around too! Then I actually projectile vomited, um . . . passion! I just had to get my video out there and share it with the world, so I posted it. And, Jade, the rest is history!" MacKenzie raved overdramatically.

I could NOT believe that girl had just confessed on national TV! I breathed a sigh of relief as I continued to watch the MacKenzie freak show.

"So, what are your future plans?!" Jade asked.

"Well, I'm open to guest appearances on all the most popular dance TV shows. My vision is to revolutionize the Internet with my cutting-edge dance art, and I think I'm on my way to accomplishing that!"

"OMG! That was SO deep!" Jade gushed. "So, can you tell us which performance artist has inspired you the most?"

"NONE of them! Most performance artists are inspired by ME!" MacKenzie bragged.

Maybe the glare from those bright camera lights had affected my eyes. But while I was watching MacKenzie's interview, her head appeared to be swelling up larger and larger!

OMG! Her EGO was so big, it had stretch marks.

I was just hoping she'd complete her interview before her head actually EXPLODED on live television!

BOOOM!!

After the TeenTV interview was over, students excitedly swarmed the halls and actually mobbed MacKenzie. . . .

MACKENZIE'S FAN CLUB

They begged her for an autograph and took selfies with her like she was a Hollywood A-list celebrity or something.

Due to MacKenzie's newfound FAME, she decided to CANCEL the meeting with Principal Winston!!

Which means I no longer have to worry about getting kicked out of school because of false allegations of cyberbullying. Since MacKenzie just confessed on national television that SHE posted the bug video, this DRAMAFEST is over!

FOREVER!!

SQUEEEEEE!!

☺!!

OMG! I feel SO relieved! It's like a ton of weight has FINALLY been lifted off my shoulders.

I actually survived the student exchange program at North Hampton Hills.

I'm STILL in the running for that fabulous trip to Paris.

That selfie-addicted DIVA, Tiffany Blaine Davenport, is out of my life FOREVER!

And MacKenzie's cyberbullying FIASCO is finally over.

But when Chloe, Zoey, and I passed by the office after lunch today, we saw the STRANGEST thing.

MacKenzie was frantically digging through the lost and found box like she'd lost her MIND! And Jessica was helping her. . . .

MACKENZIE SEARCHES FOR
HER LOST DIARY!

241

That's when I remembered that she'd LOST her leopard-print diary and NEVER found it. Which was actually MY DIARY, which she'd STOLEN from ME and disguised with a leopard-print cover (another LONG story)! At least I got it back!

Anyway, it's official! MacKenzie announced that she's transferring from NHH BACK to WCD!

I think this probably means she HATES me LESS than she HATES Tiffany.

And since her video went viral, she has resumed her throne as queen of the CCPs.

According to the latest gossip, MacKenzie and Jessica are BFFs again. They're already planning to make a Part Two of the bug video.

Unfortunately for me, MacKenzie was reassigned to the locker right next to MINE.

JUST GREAT ☹!!

MacKenzie was gone for FIVE weeks and has only been back for a few hours.

But it feels like she never LEFT!

I really hope her experiences at North Hampton Hills International Academy taught her a valuable lesson and that she'll change for the better.

But personally . . . I wouldn't hold my BREATH ☹!

I'm just happy to be back at WCD and hanging out with my friends, Chloe, Zoey, and Brandon.

And although MY life is far from perfect, I'm REALLY happy to FINALLY have it back.

WHY? Because . . .

I'm SUCH a DORK!!
☺!!

ACKNOWLEDGMENTS

Liesa Abrams Mignogna, my INCREDIBLE editorial director. Thank you for your steadfast patience and support. You have the unique ability to hear Nikki's voice even before she has spoken a word.

A special thanks to Karin Paprocki, my BRILLIANT and CREATIVE art director, and my AMAZING managing editor, Katherine Devendorf. Thanks for all that you do! Your guidance and assistance has been invaluable.

Daniel Lazar, my REMARKABLE agent at Writers House. Thanks for your friendship, for your support, and for helping Dork Diaries become an international bestseller.

A special thanks to my Team Dork staff at Aladdin/Simon & Schuster, Mara Anastas, Mary Marotta, Jon Anderson, Julie Doebler, Faye Bi, Carolyn Swerdloff, Lucille Rettino, Matt Pantoliano, Tara Grieco, Catherine Hayden, Michelle Leo, Candace McManus, Anthony Parisi, Christina Solazzo, Lauren Forte, Jenica Nasworthy, Kayley Hoffman, Matt Jackson,

Ellen Grafton, Jenn Rothkin, Ian Reilly, Christina Pecorale, Gary Urda, and the entire sales force. You guys ROCK!

To Torie Doherty-Munro at Writers House; to my foreign rights agents Maja Nikolic, Cecilia de la Campa, and Angharad Kowal; and to Deena, Zoé, Marie, and Joy—thanks for helping me Dorkify the world!

And last but not least, my supertalented coauthor, Erin; my supertalented illustrator, Nikki; Kim; Doris; and my entire family! I love you lots!

Always remember to let your inner DORK shine through!

Rachel Renée Russell is the #1

New York Times bestselling author of the blockbuster book series *Dork Diaries* and the bestselling new series *The Misadventures of Max Crumbly*.

There are thirty million copies of her books in print worldwide, and they have been translated into thirty-seven languages.

She enjoys working with her two daughters, Erin and Nikki, who help write and illustrate her books.

Rachel's message is "Always let your inner dork shine through!"

Do you love

DORK
diaries

and reading all about Nikki's
not-so-fabulous life??

Then don't miss out on the
BRAND NEW series from

Rachel Renée Russell!
featuring new dork on the block,

**MAX
CRUMBLY!**

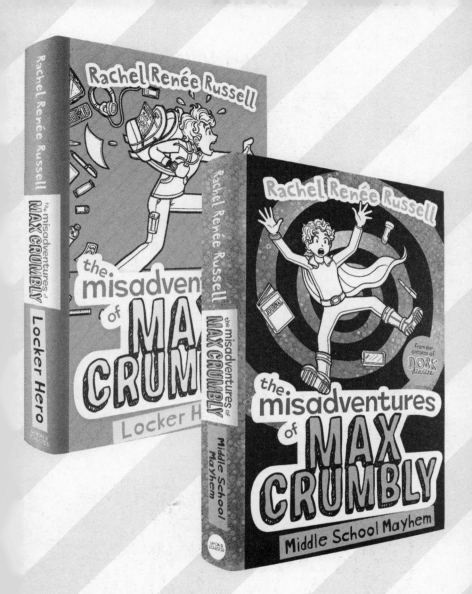

"If you like Tom Gates, Diary of A Wimpy Kid and, of course, Dork Diaries you'll love this!" *The Sun*

1. MY SECRET LIFE AS A SUPER~~HERO~~ ZERO

If I had SUPERPOWERS, life in middle school wouldn't be quite so CRUDDY.

Hey, I'd NEVER miss the stupid bus again, because I'd just FLY to school!...

AWESOME, right? That would pretty much make ME the COOLEST kid at my school!

But I'll let you in on a secret. Getting bombed by an angry bird is NOT cool. It's just . . . NASTY!!

TV, comic books, and movies make all this superhero stuff look SO easy. But it ISN'T! So don't believe the HYPE.

You CAN'T get superpowers by hanging out in a laboratory, mixing up colorful, glowing liquids that you simply DRINK....

MWA-HA-HA-HAAA!

ME, MIXING UP A YUMMY
SUPERPOWER SMOOTHIE

Let me put it this way. . . .

Even if I DID have superpowers, the very first person I'd need to rescue is . . .

MYSELF!

WHY?

Because a guy at school pulled a lousy PRANK on me.

And, unfortunately, I might be DEAD by the time you read this!

Yes, I said "DEAD."

Okay, I'll admit that he didn't MEAN to kill me.

But still . . . !!

So if you're the type who gets FREAKED OUT over this kind of stuff (or comic book cliffhangers), you probably shouldn't read my journal. . . .

Um . . . excuse me, but are you STILL reading?!

Okay, fine! Go right ahead.

Just don't say I didn't warn you!

2. IF THERE'S A DEAD BODY INSIDE MY LOCKER, IT'S PROBABLY ME!

It all started as a normal, boring, CRUMMY day in my abnormally boring, CRUMMY life.

My morning was a disaster because I overslept. Then it went straight downhill from there.

I completely lost track of time at breakfast while reading a really old comic book that my father found in the attic a few days ago.

He said his dad had given it to him as a birthday gift when he was a kid.

He warned me to be super careful with it and not take it out of the house because it was a collectible and probably worth a few hundred dollars.

My dad was pretty serious about it because he'd already scheduled an appointment to get it appraised at the local comic book store.

However, since I was running late for school, I decided to ~~sneak~~ take the comic book with me and finish reading it during lunch.

Like, what could happen to it at school?!

Anyway, as I rushed to the bus stop, the zipper broke on my backpack and all my stuff fell out, including Dad's comic book.

I was like, Oh, CRUD!! My dad is going to STRANGLE ME if I damage his comic book!

I grabbed the comic book and was desperately trying to pick up everything else when the bus pulled up, screeched to a halt, waited all of three seconds, and then zoomed off again.

Without me!

Hey, I ran after that thing like it was a $100 bill blowing in the wind!

"STOP!! STOP!! STOOOOP!" I yelled.

But it didn't.

Which meant I missed the bus, was forced to walk to school, and arrived twenty minutes late.

Next I got chewed out by the office secretary. She gave me a tardy slip and then threatened an after-school detention because I had interrupted her while she was eating a jelly doughnut.

And just when I thought things couldn't possibly get ANY worse, they did.

When I stopped by my locker to get my books, suddenly everything went DARK.

That's when I realized I was TRAPPED in my worst . . .

NIGHTMARE!

I knew attending a new middle school was going to be tough, but this is INSANE.

My life STINKS!

I know you're probably thinking, Dude, just chill! Everybody has a BAD day at school.

Stop whining and GET OVER IT!

For real?

Are you serious?

Like, HOW am I supposed to get over THIS?! ...

Doug Thurston, better known as "Thug" Thurston, just STUFFED ME INSIDE MY LOCKER!! AGAIN! And it's only the second week of school.

Are we having FUN yet? I've been crammed inside here for what seems like forever!!

And, unfortunately, I don't have my cell phone to call for help! I was in such a big rush this morning, I left it sitting right on the table after breakfast.

My legs are so numb, I could probably saw off my big toe with my metal ruler and not feel a thing. And did I mention that I just had an asthma attack? If I didn't always have my inhaler with me at school, I'd probably already be dead by now!

I'm definitely going to be dead by lunchtime due to suffocation from limited oxygen and the stench of the funky gym clothes in the locker next door.

Which is ironic when you think about it, because I should have died DURING lunch the first time I ate the SEWER SLUDGE they try to pass off as food in the cafeteria!

~~And if all of THIS isn't enough TORTURE, I have to PEE! REALLY bad!~~

I need to figure out how I'm going to get out of this stupid locker.

Luckily, I have my flashlight key chain with me. Otherwise it would be pitch-black in here.

The ONLY reason I'm writing all of this in my journal is because I'm worried that one day Thug Thurston will stuff me in my locker and I'll NEVER get out.

So I came up with an ingenious plan.

When the authorities arrive to investigate my mysterious disappearance, the FIRST thing they're going to find inside my locker ~~(after my DECOMPOSED BODY!)~~ is this journal! . . .

ME, AFTER I'M FOUND INSIDE MY
LOCKER WITH MY JOURNAL!

I'm calling it THE MISADVENTURES OF MAX CRUMBLY, and it's basically a highly detailed record of all ~~the CRAP I've had to deal with!~~ my experiences here at this school.

Since there's a chance I WON'T make it out of my locker alive, I've provided enough evidence in these pages to send Thug Thurston away to PRISON!

For LIFE!

Or at least land his butt in after-school detention every day until he graduates ~~or drops out of school, whichever comes first!~~

Hey, I'm NOT trying to save the world or be a hero or anything like that, so don't get it twisted.

But if I can prevent what happened to ME from happening to YOU or another kid, then every second I spend suffering inside my locker will be worth it.

3. HOW DARTH VADER BECAME
MY FATHER

I know some of you are probably thinking . . .

Is this guy for real? Is he actually writing all of this from INSIDE his LOCKER?

I totally understand and appreciate your skepticism.

I'M having a REALLY hard time believing all of this is actually happening to me TOO! I guess I should start by introducing myself.

My name is Maxwell Crumbly, and I'm an eighth grader at South Ridge Middle School.

But most of the kids at my school just call me ~~Barf, after I threw up my oatmeal in PE class~~ Max.

And YES! I did all these drawings myself.

Here's what I look like right now. . . .

Actually, that is probably NOT the best drawing of me. So let me try this again.

Okay, here's one that's a lot better....

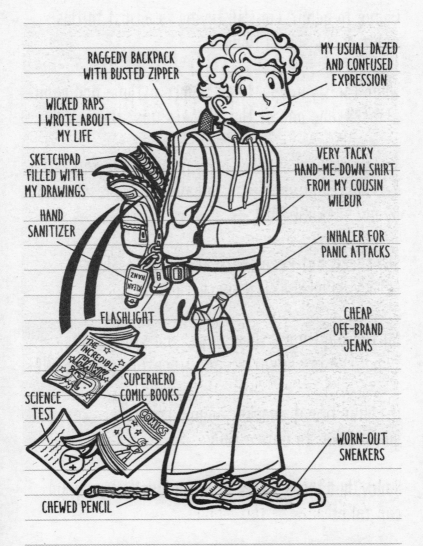

SELF-PORTRAIT OF ME (MAX CRUMBLY)

I have to admit, I'm still trying to adjust to this whole public school thing.

When I was younger, I had severe asthma and panic attacks, and one of the triggers was stress.

So for medical reasons my parents made the decision eight years ago to have me homeschooled by my GRANDMOTHER.

But that's not even the SCARIEST part. She's a retired KINDERGARTEN teacher!!

All the naptimes, sippy cups, and storybooks I endured in seventh grade were just . . . WRONG!

If I have to eat another animal cracker, I swear I'm gonna puke an entire ZOO!

Sorry, but there's only so much humiliation a kid can take.

So I secretly made plans to call Child Protective Services and report my grandma for CHILD ABUSE!

It was probably the happiest day of my life when my parents FINALLY agreed to let me attend South Ridge Middle School.

Since I'm a lot older now and on new medication, my doctor said I should be just fine.

The only complication is that if my parents find out I'm having any problem WHATSOEVER at my new school that could be stressful for me, ~~I'm gonna be stuck with Grandma, sippy cups, and naptimes until high school graduation!~~ they're going to snatch me out of this school so fast it'll make my head spin.

So I really need to fix this Thug Thurston problem. And FAST!!!

But it's kind of complicated because he's as big as an ox and kind of smells like one too.

I sit right behind him in math class, and some days it's hard for me to breathe. So I just plug my nose and mutter to myself....

ME, TRYING NOT TO BREATHE THUG'S
TOXIC BODY ODOR FUMES

Do you remember me mentioning that I have an inhaler? It provides a strong dose of medicine to help me breathe.

Well, that thing is totally USELESS against Thug!

I scrounged around our garage until I found my dad's gas mask (his hobby is painting cars). And now I wear it to class for "medical reasons" whenever Thug's STINK is abnormally PUNGENT. . . .

← ME, WEARING A GAS MASK TO CLASS

The weird thing is that Thug is really friendly to me on the days that I wear it.

WHY?

Because he actually thinks I'm DARTH VADER'S SON! I swear. I am NOT lying to you.

He told me that when he grows up he wants to go to college to become a Dark Sith Lord just like my DAD. And he said he's already saved up $3.94 toward buying a black cape, a mask, and a red lightsaber.

Definitely some CRAZY stuff, right? But it makes sense when you consider the fact that Thug has flunked eighth grade, like, THREE times!

I almost fell out of my chair when he invited ~~Darth Vader's son~~ ME over to his house for pizza and video games.

But I decided NOT to go, because at some point I was going to have to take off my mask to eat a few slices of pizza.

And when Thug FINALLY figured out I really WASN'T Darth Vader's son, he was going to beat my face into a pulp.

If I could stand to wear that mask the entire school day, I bet Thug and I could become BEST BUDS!...

THUG AND ME, HANGING OUT!

Since we're on the subject of best buds, I can count the number of friends I have ~~on one hand~~ with just one finger.

A few weeks ago I met this guy at the store Pets-N-Stuff, but he goes to Westchester Country Day Middle School. I was there buying dog food with my grandma's crazy Yorkie, Creampuff, when the little furball started yip-yapping viciously (I say that with sarcasm) and jumped out of my arms to "attack" this guy who was walking by.

"Whoa! Easy there, Killer!" he laughed. Then he dug into his pocket, pulled out a doggy treat, knelt down, and held it out. "I'm your friend! See?"

Creampuff stopped barking, and after sniffing the stranger's hand, he happily accepted the treat, wagged his tail, and then licked the guy's face.

"Dude! He's nicer to you than he is to me, and I've been feeding him and picking up his poop for five years!" I exclaimed.

"Yeah, Yorkies are a little high-strung. But they're friendly once they warm up to you," he explained.

"So, you're like the Dog Whisperer. How did you learn to be so good with dogs?" I asked.

"Actually, I spend WAY too much time with them," he laughed. "I volunteer at Fuzzy Friends Animal Rescue Center."

"I'm no dog trainer, but I can give Creampuff a bath without drowning him!" I joked. "Does Fuzzy Friends need a dog washer?"

That's how Brandon and I became good friends. He's pretty cool, and we hang out at Fuzzy Friends once a week, taking care of the dogs there.

And, unlike Thug, Brandon isn't hanging around me just because he thinks my dad is Darth Vader.

What can I say? Some people drink at the fountain of knowledge, while others (like Thug) just GARGLE and SPIT!